Jack's New Power

JACK GANTOS

JACK'S NEW POWER

Stories from a Caribbean Year

SQUARE
FISH

Farrar Straus Giroux
New York

SQUARE
FISH

An Imprint of Macmillan

Library of Congress Cataloging-in-Publication Data
Gantos, Jack.
Jack's new power / by Jack Gantos.
p.   cm.
Summary: Thirteen-year-old Jack learns that life is not always idyllic
on an island paradise when his father moves the family to Barbados.
ISBN 978-0-374-43715-2
[1. Family life—Fiction. 2. Americans—Barbados—Fiction.
3. Barbados—Fiction.] I. Title.
PZ7.G15334Jac 1995   [Fic]—dc20   94-44442

Originally published in the United States by Farrar Straus Giroux
First Square Fish Edition: December 2011
Square Fish logo designed by Filomena Tuosto
mackids.com

20 19 18 17 16 15 14

AR: 4.3 / LEXILE: 580L

For Anne

Contents

Dynasty 3

Purple 33

Love 63

New Power 83

The Pistol 117

Thurston Branch 139

Man's Man 171

Fire 195

pointed his finger at
me. "Just give the tail
a yank," Pete holle
I knew right away
this was a stu
thing to do. S
pulled the no
smelling tail

The drawing shield reads: WEAK LINK JACK

horse did not like me and kic
me so hard I lifted off the gr
and landed in a sticker br
"When I catch you I'll k
you back." But you the ki
horse was gone. The onl
left behind was a shoe
on my leg.

Dynasty

We were not allowed to swim in the ocean far below the Edgewater Hotel because we were on the rough side of the island. The "windward" side, Dad had called it. It was rugged and gusty, and the blue waves arrived in towering rows all the way from Africa. They glided across the ocean like a conquering navy and crashed against the shore, which was fortified with huge skull-shaped boulders crowned with spikes of sharp rock. The waves kept coming, but Barbados didn't budge an inch. I figured if a wave ever hurled me against one of those prickly skulls I'd be gutted like the fish we had been eating for dinner each night.

There were small inlets of pink sandy beach as smooth and soft as slices of melon, but signs everywhere warned about the undertow. And we had been lectured by Dad against going down the steps carved into the face of the coral rock to play on the beach. Just to make sure we wouldn't get near the ocean, he told us the story of the two German girls. He gathered us on the wooden balcony over-looking the shore. The wind was briny with salt spray and blew our hair and clothes to one side, so that we looked like the small, twisted trees bent toward the land.

"Come here," he hollered to the three of us. We huddled around him and watched his every move. He pulled up on the crease of his cream pants leg and lifted his brown shoe onto the lower rung of the balcony. I did the same. Pete did what I did. Betsy looked impatient and scratched a mosquito bite on her ankle.

He removed a cigarette from his case and tapped the filter against the face of his watch. Then, in one quick motion, he snapped open his lighter and shielded the flame with his free hand as he drew in a breath so deep his cheeks pressed against his teeth and bones like a mummy. Dad was warming up to telling a really good story.

"All Germans can read English," he started, and raised a finger to mark his first point. "But the girls ignored the red warning signs and were swept out to sea by the undertow." He pointed to the breakers, which slapped and fanned over the beach, then receded into the bottom of the following wave. "Still, they got a second chance. A Canadian father and son were on the shore and spotted them as they desperately waved their arms for help. 'Stick with me,' the father said to his son. They bravely dove into the water, but the son couldn't keep up. They never reached the girls and the girls never reached the shore. The father was also dragged out to sea. Only the son was washed back onto the beach. You can imagine just how that boy felt for not staying by his father's side."

I did imagine. He would have dropped to his knees on the shore and pounded his chest with his fists while the waves washed up over him. Somehow, I figured, the father was punished because the son was weak. I promised to do everything my father asked of me. Never again would I lie or cheat or misbehave. I'd be strong and brave and smart. I looked over at Pete. He had covered his eyes with one hand. I could tell he was thinking the same thing I was: Stick with Dad. Don't let him down.

Dad continued. "A week later, what was left of the three bodies washed ashore on Crane Beach, some twelve miles away. The sharks had gotten to them first, then the crabs. You can just imagine how horrid they were," he whispered and gazed dreamily out to sea. "They looked like bloated lepers." He took a quick pull on his cigarette, then flicked it over the balcony. The wind blew it back against the cliff. He bowed his head in respect for the dead.

"I think they get the message," Mom piped in just as I was forming a spongy, rotting picture of "bloated lepers" in my mind. She had crept up on us for the gruesome ending. I stared at the maroon paisley scarf she had fixed around her head to keep her hair in place. With the spooky mood I was in, each paisley design looked like a thick dollop of blood.

Dad snapped out of his daze and curled his arm around Mom's waist. "We'll be in the lounge if you need us," he announced with a sudden new energy. The lesson was over.

"You all play by the pool," Mom ordered. "Betsy, keep an eye on the boys. You know how they get."

That was one of the differences between Dad and Mom. Dad could get us worked up to do anything he wanted by telling us a lesson story with a tragic ending. Mom just went right to the point and told us what to do. Even though she was pushier, he was more convincing.

Pete and I ran up to our room. We didn't have to share it with Betsy, who was stuck with the baby. This meant we could wrestle and make all the noise we wanted and sneak out at night to raid the bar for bottles of lemon soda.

We had been living at the Edgewater Hotel for a week. Dad had flown down from Fort Lauderdale a month before us. When we joined him, our house wasn't ready, so he checked us into the Edgewater because it was close to where he was fixing up a large private track club called the Round House. He took us to see it. It was the most beautiful building I had ever seen. It was pure white and sparkled with "diamond-dust plaster," as Dad put it. The walls were round as a cake, and it had an orange tin roof as tall and pointy as a party hat. There was a little red flag in the shape of a horse sticking out the top. The driveway gravel was pink and reminded me of candy hearts. I picked up a piece and licked it. If it had tasted sweet it would prove we were living in a fairy tale. It tasted like clean dust and I spit it out. It really didn't bother me that we weren't living in a fairy tale. Living on Barbados was pretty close.

We threw our clothes off and pulled our new bathing trunks up over our skinny white legs. After we knotted the drawstrings inside our waistbands, we ran down to the pool. Betsy had settled on a lounge chair to read a book.

The baby was asleep in his carriage under a striped umbrella with fringe around the edges.

Pete and I gathered up a garden hose, a big rock, and my swim mask. We were playing a game we called "Deep-Sea Diver" after a movie we had seen in the television room. I was the diver and Pete was my air-pump and support crew. Anyone who dove into the pool would be a giant squid. If they touched me, I was strangled to death.

I put on my mask, stuck one end of the hose in my mouth, picked up the rock, and jumped into the deep end. I held my breath and sank to the bottom. I exhaled out of the corner of my mouth and watched the silver-and-blue bubbles go all the way up to the blurry surface. Then I breathed through the hose. It worked. There was air flowing through. I exhaled and took a deep breath. Then I held the hose with my right hand and tugged on it twice. That was the signal. In a moment I could taste lemon soda mixed with some funky inner-hose scum. Then there was more soda, and more. I needed to breathe. I pulled on the hose. The soda slowed to a trickle, then stopped.

This was great. I could have stayed there the entire day. Pete could feed me olives, raisins, and little Vienna sausages all washed down with my new favorite soda, Lemon Squash.

I was thinking that the air was getting a little thin and it would be a good idea if we had a bicycle pump to hook on to the hose so Pete could pump fresh air to me. Suddenly the hose was jerked out of my mouth and I swallowed a lungful of water. I pushed the rock to one side and sprang up toward the surface. "Why'd you do that?" I sputtered.

"Come quick," Pete said and pranced up and down on his toes as if he had to pee. "Dad's drowning."

I dragged myself up over the stone edge of the pool and grabbed a towel as we ran toward the lounge. No one was inside. They were all out on the back balcony, peering down toward the rocks and rolling ocean and pointing at two tiny heads bobbing up and down over the huge swells. I could tell right away that with each passing wave they were drawn closer and closer to the prickly rocks. In a few minutes they'd be dead, pinned to the sharp spikes like prize butterflies. I also knew that neither of them was Dad. He wasn't even in the water yet.

He was running across the beach. Without slowing, he pulled his shirt over his head, kicked off his shoes, unbuckled his trousers and hopped out of them, and waded into the water. He dove forward and began to swim. His arms and legs kicked up whitewater as he raced to reach the couple before they struck the rocks. It was going to be close.

"He's going to die!" Betsy screamed. She was scared and angry. "Stop him! He's insane!"

"He'll be okay," Mom said, and took a deep breath. She stood behind Betsy and held her shoulders. "He's a good swimmer."

He was. When we had lived on Cape Hatteras, he swam in the ocean all the time, right next to the signs warning everyone about the undertow. I was small then and thought undertow meant that if you stuck your toe into the water you got pulled under and drowned. It wasn't quite like that. What it meant was that if you were swimming close to the shore a current of water could pull you straight out to sea and keep you from swimming back in. It didn't

pull you under, but eventually you got tired and drowned.
I knew there was only one way to beat an undertow. Once
it carried you out to sea, you had to swim parallel to the
shoreline for a while and then head in to the beach. That
way, you swam beyond the control of the undertow current and lived to tell about it.

"He knows what he's doing," I said to Pete. "Watch
him."

Pete covered his eyes and peeked between his fingers.
He still hadn't learned to swim and was terrified of the
water.

"He's not even getting tired," I said, elbowing Pete.
"Keep your eyes open, you'll learn something."

Just then Betsy fell out of Mom's grip and slumped to
the floor. As soon as she landed on her rear, she hopped
up and started screaming and swinging her arms.

"She's hysterical," said the bartender. "I'll get her a
brandy." He ran off and returned with a golden drink and
poured it down her throat. She spit most of it right out, but
it worked. She stood on her own two feet and stopped
struggling. Mom stroked her hair and quietly whispered in
her ear. Someone brought a blanket and draped it over her
shoulders.

Dad was still going strong. He swam up the swells, then
down into the gullies, then up again, until he had almost
reached them. And then he stopped. They were about
twenty feet from the neck of an enormous rock with points
as sharp as swords. All around its base was a circle of foam
where the waves had surged up against it and angrily slid
down.

He wanted to calm the couple before making his move.

He made a lot of hand gestures, then went forward with his plan. He swam up to the woman, turned her onto her back, and held her across the chest before she could struggle. Once he got her into position, he did a sidestroke and slowly angled down the beach and away from the undertow. The man followed. Stroke by stroke they pulled away from the rocks as the swells curled beneath them.

A group of men and women scurried down the steps to the beach, forming a human chain into the water.

"Can I go, too?" I asked Mom.

"No," she replied. "You kids stay up here with me." Dad had also told us all another true ocean story. Two children and their parents were on a small sailboat in a storm. The wife was hit by the swinging boom and knocked overboard. She went straight down into the dark water. The father tried to jump overboard to save her, but the children grabbed him and held him back. They could live with one missing parent, but not two. They would never know if the father could have saved the mother.

Mom didn't want to lose more than one. But she wouldn't have to. Dad had gone far enough downshore and had turned toward the beach. There was no undertow running against him. The waves carried him forward. The swells turned into breakers and they rode in as if on white horses. The chain of people grew longer and in a minute they had him. Then the woman. Then the man.

Two men dragged Dad ashore, where he sat slumped forward, with his head resting between his knees. Finally, once he got his breath back, he looked up at us and waved.

We waved back, wildly. I was so proud of him. He was

a hero. No one else risked his life to save that couple. Even if someone had, he would have drowned. But Dad was fearless. I knew I couldn't have done what he did. But since he was my dad, it was almost the same thing. After all, I was named after him. I was a chip off the old block . . . If he could do it, I could do it.

A circle of men and women gathered around him and helped him to his feet. Then the entire procession climbed the steps and appeared up over the cliff. Betsy threw off her blanket and ran at him with her arms open. He picked her up and swung her over his head, then back to the floor, where she pressed her face into his chest.

Pete and I took a hand each as Mom kissed his face and smoothed his hair.

"Drinks for everyone," Dad announced, his eyes flashing around the room. He was in good spirits. He pulled his hand from my grasp and swung around to point at the couple he saved. They were gone. Everyone fanned out to find them, but they had vanished. I stared out at the ocean to see if they had gone back in. Maybe they wanted to drown themselves like mysterious lovers who throw themselves off a cliff.

"Well, whoever they are," Dad said with a quick laugh, "put it *all* on their bill."

Everyone cheered.

By the end of the evening, the only thing we knew about the couple was that they were British, were on their honeymoon, and, as Dad put it, "were as dumb as dirt for swimming in water that could flip a battleship."

In the morning, they had checked out.

·　·　·

Two days later we were sitting at dinner when the waiter brought Dad a cable. He ripped the envelope down the side and removed the message.

"Well, what do you know," he said after a moment. "I saved some British royalty."

"Let's see," Betsy said, squealing, and snatched the cable from his hand.

"Read it out loud," said Mom.

"SORRY TO HAVE RUN OFF STOP COULDN'T HAVE PRESS INVOLVED STOP EVERY MEMBER OF OUR FAMILY THANKS YOU AND YOUR FAMILY STOP WHEN IN ENGLAND CONTACT LORD AND LADY JEFFRIES DUKE AND DUCHESS OF SUSSEX STOP 01-704-9776 ETERNALLY GRATEFUL." She lowered the cable and sighed.

"Now, that is what I call a happy ending," Dad said.

Mom didn't think so. "I call it rude," she pitched in. She was still annoyed because Dad had risked his life and they didn't have the manners to say thank you to his face.

"Can we call the number?" Betsy asked.

"We'll see," Dad replied.

"I'd love to be British," Betsy said, swooning. "They are so great. Every family has so much history to them. Like the Duke of Marlborough. Or the Viceroy of Firth. Or the Duchess of Windsor. And then there's us. The Henry family. Now, that does *not* sound like greatness."

"Wait a minute," Dad cut in. "We're Americans and we build great families the American way."

Betsy raised her eyebrows. "And how might that be?"

"First," he replied, "Americans don't have royal families. We have business families, political dynasties, powerhouse sports families. Americans don't have to be *born* into greatness. We can *make* ourselves great. That's the American way."

Betsy smirked. "The American way is nothing but a rat race. I'd rather win the lottery and move to Europe."

I was staying out of this discussion. Somehow I knew it would lead to something bad. I stared up at the dining-room walls. Just below the ceiling beams were a series of British coats of arms in the shape of little shields. On the shields were pictures of lions and eagles and fearless men in armor and words such as *honour, courage, wisdom*. The British used to own Barbados and had left a lot of their old stuff behind once the island gained independence. It would be neat, I thought, to have a Henry Family coat of arms.

Dad's voice became louder. "All great families begin their road to greatness by facing their fears. So that's how we'll begin." Suddenly he pointed his butter knife at my nose. "Jack, what's your greatest fear?"

My mouth was filled with a huge chunk of bread. Mom, Betsy, and Pete turned to look at me. I couldn't say a word. I just chewed and chewed. For a moment I thought my greatest fear was choking to death.

"Take your time," Dad said warmly, giving me room. "Dig deep inside yourself and think of something that gives you the shivers, really makes you break out in a cold sweat and want to run away like a coward. Well? Come on. Time's up. What's it going to be?"

I swallowed hard. " 'orses," I managed to mutter.

"Huh? Speak up," Dad insisted, leaning closer. "Don't be so afraid that you can't even say it."

I took a quick sip of water and swallowed. "Horses," I said. "I'm afraid of horses."

Dad made a face. "Is that it?"

"Yeah," I replied. "I'm afraid of being kicked by a horse."

"Well, that's a beginning," he said. "Once you get over that, we'll move on to something more important."

He turned toward Pete. I sighed and thought of standing behind a horse and having it kick me on the forehead with a ten-pound steel shoe attached to its deadly back hoof. Just the thought of it made my shoulders flinch.

Pete had taken advantage of the two minutes it took me to ruin myself.

"Water," he blurted out and started to twist his face up in a panic. "I can't swim."

"We'll fix that," Dad announced and waved his fork as though it were a magic wand. I half expected Pete to jump up, run across the dining room to the patio, dive into the pool, and swim like a dolphin.

"Betsy?" Dad said. "Let's hear it."

"Okay," she replied. She had used the time to organize exactly what was on her mind. "I'm afraid I'll call the number on this cable and they'll ask me who I am, and who I know, and who were my ancestors, and I'll tell them we are the Henry family and they'll reply, 'Henry? Are you servants? We don't recall any Henry family.' And they'll hang up because we are a bunch of nobodies."

There was a long pause while Dad leaned back in his chair. He gazed up at the ceiling and breathed deeply. Then more deeply. It seemed as though all the air in the room, the curtains, the tablecloth corners, the little table flowers, all nodded toward his flaring nostrils. After a moment, he exhaled and looked Betsy directly in the eyes.

"We are not a bunch of *nobodies*," he said. "I know we're

starting over here and we don't have some long family history filled with snotty blue bloods. But that's not what is important. We are a family at the beginning of greatness. All those British royalty had to come from somewhere. At some point they were living in caves, wearing animal skins, and beating each other with sticks. So, big deal, they've had a head start on us. Now they're at the butt end of their empire and we are at the beginning of ours. And, for my money, I'd rather be part of something new and great than be some royal has-been."

"Honey," Mom whispered. "Keep your voice down. We don't want to cause a scene." There were a lot of British guests at the hotel.

Betsy lowered her head. She had taken it too far. There were times when she could beat him in an argument. But there were also times when he reared back and let her have it. He had just nailed her.

"So," he said, wrapping up his point, "you can face your fear and give them a call."

I felt like an idiot for revealing my fear of horses. A call would be easy to make. I should have said I had a fear of something like spending money. Then Dad could give me a bundle and let me face my fear by letting me go on a spending spree.

He turned toward Mom.

She put on a cheerful face and saved the mood of the dinner. "No doubt about it," she said. "Driving a car is my greatest fear. And now with the baby I'll be trapped if I don't learn to drive."

Dad nodded. "Very good," he said with a jolly voice. "I'll get you a car and lessons."

"What about the baby?" I asked.

"He's exempt until he's three," Dad replied. "Then he has to join the *rat race* like the rest of us." He propped his elbows on the table and narrowed his eyes. "We'll start tomorrow."

But Betsy wasn't finished. "What's your fear?" she asked, still trying to corner him. "Everyone has something they're afraid of. Even you!"

He tucked in his chin and stared out at us. "My fear," he said, "is that you all will let me down."

In the morning Dad came into our room. He woke Pete and me. "I've been thinking how to conquer fear," he said. "It's a combination of dread and encouragement.

"Jack," he ordered, "you'll help Pete build up his confidence today. Give him some easy lessons. Show him how you swim. All he needs is encouragement."

"Okay," I replied. I looked over at Pete and gave him our brothers-for-life wink.

"I'll provide the dread," Dad said, and sat down on the corner of the bed. "Listen to this. I knew a man once who was a great big guy. Huge. Big arms, big legs. All muscle and not afraid of a thing. But his son was afraid of the water. Couldn't get near the stuff without shaking all over like a girl. The father tried everything to teach the boy about the water. YMCA swim lessons. Swim camp. The whole thing. Finally he got frustrated. He picked up the boy and put him in a speedboat and roared off into the harbor. He pulled up to a buoy and set the boy on the little floating platform. 'You'll either swim in or you'll starve to death out here,' he growled, and roared off. And you know what?"

Dad paused.

"He starved," whispered Pete, with his face all white and his hand over his eyes as he imagined the boy on the buoy.

Dad grabbed Pete by the head and gave him an Indian rub with his unshaven chin. Then he let him loose. "No, knucklehead. The boy swam to shore. He could swim all along. He was just being *stubborn!*"

"But I'm afraid," Pete said.

Dad had reached his limit. He stood up. "Jack will help you swim. Just as you'll help him with his fear of horses." Then he left.

Pete dropped onto the floor and peeked up at me like a kitten about to be drowned.

"I'll help you," I said. "We can't let him down."

"And I'll help you with the horses," he replied. "I'm not so scared of them."

After breakfast I wanted to get started but Pete refused.

"You can't swim on a full stomach," he said. "Let's do the horses first."

He was right. "Okay. But let's just get it over with."

Horseback riding was advertised in the hotel brochure. There were stables and long horse trails cut through the brush and trees on the land side of the hotel.

We had started down the footpath to the stables when Pete said, "Stop, I have to tell you a story of dread before I give you encouragement."

"I have enough dread," I said, groaning.

"We have to play by the rules." Pete sat down on the path. "I won't help unless you listen."

I sat next to him.

"Once there was a boy named Alexander. His father owned a huge horse and everyone who tried to ride it was thrown off and killed. Alexander's father said that if anyone could tame the horse they could have it. Everyone who had tried to ride the horse faced it toward the sun. So Alexander faced the horse away from the sun. Then he jumped on the horse and rode away. When his father saw what he had done, he gave him the horse and called him Alexander the Great."

I glared at Pete. "You're scaring me because I can't figure out what you mean," I said. "Where's the dread?"

"I mean that if you use your brains you can win. Horses aren't very smart."

"They don't need brains," I said. "They're killers."

We walked down to the stable. A short, heavy man named Mr. Doobie cared for the horses. I figured he was an old jockey who'd retired to eating.

"I got a nice one," he muttered, and pointed to a dark, nervous giant. Its eyes were like polished stones. "He used to be a racehorse at the track down below until his accident." He pointed at a two-foot jagged scar running down the animal's neck. "He can be a little moody if he don't sleep well. He still has nightmares of that picket fence."

I hoped he'd had a good night's sleep. His name was Winny and he was wearing a Western saddle, which I liked because it would give me something to hang on to. Still, as soon as I got close to Winny my fear of him made me weak. When he shuddered and waved his big head from side to side and snorted, I jumped back a few steps. His hind leg twitched and I was sure he wanted to kick me into the water trough.

Pete wasn't impressed. "Horses know when you are afraid of them. Just treat 'em like big dogs."

Finally, he had said something dreadful. I also had a huge fear of big dogs.

"Are you afraid of riding horses?" Pete asked.

"I'm more afraid of being kicked in the head," I said.

"Then let's conquer your greatest fear, like Dad said. If you get over being kicked, then riding them will be a breeze." He took the bridle and walked the horse down the path and away from the sun. I waited until he had gone about twenty feet before I followed. When he stopped, I stopped.

"Come here," Pete said. He pulled his T-shirt up over his head. "Tie this around your eyes."

I did.

"Give me your hand."

I held it out. He clutched it and pulled me along. I hadn't covered my ears very well and heard the horse pawing the ground and shuddering.

"Now stand here," he said.

I stood as stiff as a pillar. With each breath I smelled the horse and figured it smelled my fear. I felt the ground move as it tramped up and down. I could sense it was lining me up for a world-class kick. I gritted my teeth and waited for the blow.

"Reach your left hand straight out," Pete ordered.

I did. I touched the horse and instinctively pulled back.

"Just do what I say and you'll be fine. Now stick out your hand."

I extended it, slowly. I felt horsehair and the roundness of his rump. I lifted my hand just so it hovered over the horse. I didn't want to disturb it.

"Move your hand down until you feel the tail," Pete ordered.

Slowly, I lowered my hand until I felt the long, coarse hairs.

"Now gently grab the tail."

I did.

"Now give it a little tug."

I froze.

"Just a little tug," he insisted. "Then you won't have to do any more and I'll tell Dad you conquered your fear."

I took a deep breath and yanked the tail as though I were pulling a bell rope. The horse kicked me so viciously in the thigh that I skipped across the ground, staggered up the dirt path, and collapsed sideways into the bushes. The horse galloped off as I reached up with my free arm and jerked the shirt over my head.

Pete was laughing so hard he had dropped onto his knees. When he saw me staring at him, he stood up and backed away.

"I'll kill you! I'll murder you!" I shouted. "No, I won't murder you. I'll drown you! I'll make you go deep-sea diving without a hose. You'll do more than face your fear. You'll face your Maker!"

"I was just trying to help," he cried. "You faced your fear and you survived. It wasn't that bad."

I may have survived, but my fear had multiplied. I

untangled myself from the bush and put all my weight on my leg. It held. It wasn't broken, but it throbbed. I undid my belt and dropped my pants. There was a red horseshoe-shaped bruise glowing on my swollen thigh. I could even see where the nail heads had made little circles on my skin. The horse had branded me. It owned me. I pulled my pants up.

"You're dead," I said, and began to limp up the path. "Just return the horse to the stable before I drown you."

I needed to lie down.

Pete didn't wait for me to drown him. After I rested my leg, I put on my bathing suit and went down to the pool. He was in the shallow end with a Styrofoam bubble strapped to his back and little plastic water wings on his arms. He couldn't sink if I sat on him.

"Hey," I said. "You're doing great."

He turned and smiled up at me. "Thanks," he sputtered and thrashed his arms around. "I was so afraid you'd drown me I started without you."

Dad was right. Fear of one thing can really get a person to face the fear of another thing altogether.

I stepped into the water and waded over to him. "Okay," I instructed. "I'll hold you up as you swim from side to side. But first you have to take off the water wings."

"I keep the bubble on," he insisted.

"Okay."

"Sorry about the horse," he said. "I was just doing my best."

"You'll notice," I said, "that I am not asking you to practice in the *deep* end. What you did to me was like pushing a blind man into traffic so he could get over his fear of cars. Now let's go."

I held him under the belly as he began to swim the crawl with his legs kicking and his arms flailing. Then I unsnapped the clip on his bubble and stepped away.

"Excuse me," I shouted above his splashing. "I forgot to tell you a story of dread. Once upon a time there was a demented older brother with a horseshoe branded on his leg . . ."

He finally noticed he was alone. "Help," he gurgled.

"You need help holding your breath?" I asked, and pushed him under. I counted to three, then hauled him up.

"Help!"

"Who is the boss?" I asked.

"You are."

"Who is the master?"

"You are."

I led him over to the edge. "Tomorrow I'll teach you the fine points of swimming," I said.

He grabbed the edge of the pool and held on. Now he had plenty of dread.

When we sat down to dinner, everyone seemed to be smiling except for me.

"Well," Dad started. "I didn't tell you this last night. I didn't want to jinx myself by talking about it. But I was afraid that my bid on a hotel renovation might not be accepted. I thought I had bid too high. And without that job I would have let all of you down. But I found out this morning that the bid was accepted, and I'll be working close to where we'll be living on the other side of the island. The job is good for at least half a year."

Mom leaned over and gave him a kiss. "Congratulations, honey," she said. He beamed.

Pete was next. "I did some swimming," he blurted out.

"Good work, son," Dad replied. "I knew I wouldn't have to drop you off on a buoy."

"And I did some driving," Mom chirped, and nodded approvingly at herself.

"But you've always been terrified of driving," I said. I was really counting on her not to face her fear. "And the drivers here are insane."

"I know. But your dad told me a little story that really hit home."

"What's that?" I asked.

Mom glanced at Dad.

"You tell him," Dad replied and nodded.

"It was back in Fort Lauderdale. There was a woman who had a baby that was choking on a leaf. She couldn't unblock the baby's throat. There was a second car in the garage but she didn't know how to drive. She called the fire department but they couldn't get there right away. The hospital was only about ten blocks down the road and so in a panic she grabbed the baby and began to run. But the baby died in her arms just as she reached the emergency-room doors. If she had known how to drive, she would have saved that baby's life. When your dad reminded me of that story, I knew I couldn't let something like that happen to any of you kids, so I got in one of the staff cars with the chef and we practiced driving in a straight line up and down the service road."

"Very impressive," Betsy said and clapped politely. "And, believe it or not, even I have something to report."

"What?" I spit out. "What?" I could feel the world slowly closing in on me and my horse fear. I was going to be the only loser.

"Before I tell you, I want to apologize to Dad for talking the way I did last night. I was wrong to be so critical of us all."

What was wrong with her? She must have been turned into a zombie overnight. She never apologized for anything in her life. *Never!*

"It happens to the best of 'em," Dad said with a chuckle. "Now, what's your news."

"Well, after that little story you told me," she said, nodding toward Dad, "I faced my fear. I called the British couple you saved and told them who I was. And they were really nice. They said you were a hero and they'd told all their close friends about this great American man who saved them and they apologized over and over for not thanking you in person but they weren't supposed to be on Barbados since they told their snoopy families that they were going to Italy because they wanted some privacy from the hundreds of royal relatives that would want to join them on their *honeymoon.*"

"See," Dad said proudly. "If you hadn't called, you wouldn't have known the truth of the matter."

"What story did you tell Betsy to get her going?" I asked.

Dad smiled at Betsy. She turned toward me. "Dad told

me about his older sister who had a big crush on a man named Harvey Jacobs from the rich side of town. She never told him she liked him, because she was from the poor side of the tracks. She ended up marrying someone she didn't like as much. After the wedding, her new husband said to her, Boy, I feel lucky to be married to you because Harvey Jacobs has been in love with you forever. So if she had had the courage to call Harvey Jacobs and tell him how she felt, she would be with her true love and not with some yokel she settled for. The lesson is, if you don't have the guts to ask, you'll never find out what people think of you."

I'll never have to read another book for the rest of my life, I thought. I just have to hang around Dad all day and I'll hear a story on every subject known to man. But where was mine, I wondered. What could he possibly tell me that would get me over my horse fear?

Then very slowly I could feel everyone turning their eyes on me.

"Jack, do you have anything to tell us about your day?" Dad asked.

I looked at Pete. He was sucking on a lime wedge. He had a story to tell, but he kept it to himself.

"Can I talk to you about this later?" I asked. "I'm not feeling well."

"Certainly," Mom said.

I pushed my chair back and limped out of there as quickly as I could. I went to my room and sat on my bed. I imagined our coat of arms, which would be passed down to future generations. There will be a picture of Mom driving a car. Under the picture will be the word *Bravery*. Dad will be painted standing on top of a pile of money that spells out the word *Success*. Betsy will be wearing a little royal crown and under the picture will be *Courage*. Pete will be pictured leaping off a high diving board above the word *Fearless*. Then there will be me. I'll be shown being trampled by a horse above the words *Weak Link*.

I stood up and looked into the mirror. I wanted to scare myself. "Weak link," I jeered at my reflection. "Weak link." After a moment my reflection whined back. "I can live with that."

Just then Dad came into the room.

"After you left the table Pete told us he tried to give you some encouragement. Said it didn't work."

"It backfired," I said.

"Well, I could tell you a story that would point out how facing your horse fears would make you a better man. But instead of making up a story, I'd just rather tell you the truth."

He sat down and draped his arm across my shoulders. I had a feeling that the truth was going to be scarier than a story.

"Simply put," he stated, "you can't fail. I won't allow it. You are named after me. If you fail, it's like me failing. If I hadn't saved that couple, I wouldn't be able to look you in the eyes. If you can't ride that horse, you won't be able to look me in the eyes. And a son that can't look his father in the eyes is a coward. And if we can't look each other in the eyes we will go through life like strangers."

"I'll try my best," I said.

"I've got great faith that there will be a happy ending to

this story," he said. "If you get weak-kneed, just think of me diving into that ocean. It takes courage to be a man." He slapped me on my swollen thigh, stood up, and left the room.

When I woke up the next morning I didn't even open my eyes. I could hear the wind and rain beating against the windows. It was a day to avoid horses. It was a day to avoid Dad's eyes. It was a day to avoid mirrors.

I opened my bedside drawer and pulled out my diary. I held it up to the key around my neck and unlocked it. One of the big differences between me and Dad was that he talked all his stories out. I wrote mine down. But since arriving in Barbados I hadn't written a word.

This was a good day to get caught up. I started with the story of the German girls drowning. Then I wrote about Dad being a hero. I wrote down everyone's fears. Then I wrote Dad's stories about the boy on the buoy, the choking baby, and the woman who settled for the wrong man.

But there was one story that wasn't his. It was mine. I wrote the first half of my horse story. The ending would have to wait until I had lived it.

Suddenly I was starved. I had skipped breakfast but was ready for lunch. I went down to the dining room. Pete was eating a club sandwich and French fries. I sat next to him and picked off his plate.

"Once upon a time," he started, "there was a boy who tried to eat an apple in front of a horse. But it was the horse's apple. So, when the boy wasn't looking, the horse bit off his hand." He dropped his sandwich and tried to bite me on the wrist. I yanked my arm back and smacked him hard with a straight right to his shoulder. It knocked him off his chair.

"I'm just trying to help," he hollered from the floor.

"You're driving me nuts," I yelled back. I grabbed a handful of fries and ran to the back of the hotel to be by myself.

The rain had stopped, so I went down to the stable and asked Mr. Doobie to saddle up Winny.

"I think he's in a good mood today," he speculated.

"How do you know?"

"He always liked a sloppy track."

"Oh." I had zero understanding of what horses liked or disliked.

While Mr. Doobie strapped the saddle on Winny, I worked on my story. Once upon a time there was a boy who was so afraid of horses that he wouldn't go near them. His father insisted that he try. And so one day he did. But . . .

"All set?" Mr. Doobie asked.

I just stood there. I wasn't certain what to do. But I had to do something. My story needed an ending.

"I saw where Winny gave you a kick yesterday," he said.

He was neither sympathetic nor critical, but I was embarrassed that he knew. I must have looked foolish to him.

"I once saw a jockey get kicked in the head. He had bent over to pick up a riding crop. Killed him instantly. Fell over like a three-legged chair."

"Well, it only grazed me," I replied. "It was just a game I was playing with my brother."

"Dangerous game," he remarked sharply. "I wouldn't do it again. Kinda like playing with a gun. There is no need to shoot yourself to see if it will work." He reached into his pocket, pulled out a small brown bottle, and took a swig. I hoped he didn't share that stuff with the horse.

I had heard enough stories and bits and pieces of happy and sad endings. Nothing anyone said was going to change how I felt. I had to face this fear myself.

I walked up to the horse and put one foot in the stirrup and swung my other leg up over the saddle.

The horse started to walk sideways like a crab, then forward. I grabbed the saddle horn with both hands and dropped the reins. I thought that letting go of the reins would be like putting on the brakes. It was more like pressing on the gas.

"Just hang on," Mr. Doobie shouted as I pulled away. "He'll do the rest."

Winny took off in a trot. I held on as I bounced up and down. I leaned forward with my chest on the back of his neck and grabbed the reins. "Whoa, boy. Whoa." I yanked them back.

He didn't listen. The saddle smacked my rear end with a jolt that ran up my spine and rattled my teeth. I stood up in the stirrups and pressed my knees together. Winny continued to trot.

After a few minutes I got into the clip-clop rhythm, but I couldn't stop Winny and I couldn't steer him left or right. He had his own destination in mind and I just hung on. But as long as I was on top of him, he couldn't kick me.

The road turned and went down between two small hills. As soon as I saw the point of the orange roof with the horse flag on top I knew where Winny was heading. He was going back to the track behind the Round House to face his fear of picket fences.

The road curled to the left and we started up the driveway. The pink gravel crunched under his hoofs.

Dad was examining a set of blueprints on a plywood table when he heard me. He looked up and waved. I smiled and pulled back on the reins. To my surprise, Winny came to a stop.

"Need some help?" he called out.

"No," I said. "He's just getting used to me." I threw my right leg up over the saddle and hopped down like a seasoned cowboy.

Dad was standing on the other side of the horse. I could walk either in front of Winny or behind him. There was no choice. I had to go for complete victory. If Dad was going to use me for one of his lesson stories I had to give him a dramatic finish. I could imagine him telling a friend the story of my short life. "And then the boy walked behind the horse to embrace his father, but before he could reach him, the horse reared back and kicked and the boy's head exploded as if he had walked into a spinning propeller."

"A tragedy," the friend would reply.

But I lived to give him a happy ending. I walked right behind Winny and slapped him hard on his rear. He took off like a rabbit. I stuck out my hand. "Shake," I said to Dad, and looked him directly in the eyes.

"You bet," he said happily, and clasped my hand with his.

and the only good
thing about being
purple is that when I
drink grape juice I c
spill it down my cl

NAIME

ANTHAM

P

B   J

HENRY

NELSON ROAD

HUN

FO

the other cool
when I sweat little purple drops of

Purple

I had just returned from Bayley Clinic when Betsy heard me sneaking down the hall. She whipped open her bedroom door and pointed her finger directly at my swollen, purple nose.

"Don't take another step toward me," she said as she shook her head in disgust. "It's bad enough that we're new on this street, but having a purple brother is only going to make people avoid us even more. Please," she begged. "Don't go outside. Just give me a chance to make friends before the neighbors find out I'm related to a purple freak."

"It's not my fault," I replied. "It's medicine."

"You brought this on yourself," she snapped. "I told you that disgusting chicken-chasing game was going to make you sick. Before long, you'll be crowing at the sunrise and pecking the ground."

"It wasn't the chickens," I protested. "You don't know *everything*."

"Then what?" she shot back. "What?"

"It was the wart."

"The only wart you have is throbbing inside your skull," she said sarcastically.

"Well, I bet I make a new friend here before you do," I yelled and lunged at her.

She cringed. "You'll never make a friend. You're a freak of nature."

Pete came around the corner and held his nose. I smelled like vinegar. I crossed him off my buddy list. "Pete doesn't count as a new friend," I said, setting the rules. "He's just a pest."

"You're on, wart boy," Betsy replied. "But I warn you. If you come snooping around when I'm trying to make friends, I'll call the center for disease control and have you quarantined."

She probably could, I looked so bad. But I was telling the truth about the wart and she knew it. The wart was just the start of my disease. Now I had Day-Glo purple circles painted on my arms and legs. My belly was purple. My face, my ears, my neck, and even where people couldn't see me, I was purple. I had broken out in little pink blisters and boils and the nurse had painted me with Gentian Violet, which was so bright Pete put on his sunglasses to look at me.

"I am not a freak," I declared. "Mom!" I shouted.

"He's not a freak," Mom said matter-of-factly and scooted past me. I thought she could have put her arm around me and given me a motherly hug instead of treating me like a mutant. But she was wearing a white dress, and I was still a bit sticky. "He's sick," Mom said and placed her hand over her heart. "You should be thankful that it is just blood poisoning and not *leukemia.* Now leave him alone."

"With pleasure," Betsy said and marched into the kitchen.

I retreated to my room and closed the door. I hated being purple. It was the most embarrassing thing that had ever happened to me. I knew I was supposed to feel thankful that I didn't have leukemia, but when I examined myself in the mirror, I was horrified. Betsy was right. I would never make new friends. Who would want to play with a purple kid? I took off my T-shirt and shorts. I opened my closet and took out a long-sleeved shirt and jeans. I put them on and pulled a Pittsburgh Pirates cap down over my head. I glanced into the mirror again. I looked like a well-dressed grape. I wished I had a ski mask to cover my face. I took out my diary and began to write down what was happening to me. It was all pretty weird.

My purple trouble had started five days before, when our housekeeper, Marlene, taught us how to play "Chase the Chicken." She called Pete and me into the back yard and stood us next to a tree stump. In one hand she held a chicken upside down by its feet. In the other hand she gripped a machete that was so shiny under the hot sun it made me squint. "Your mother wishes chicken for supper," she said. On a tree branch just behind her head, a second chicken hung upside down from a twine handle tied around its feet. It clucked.

"Are you lads ready?" Marlene asked. She sounded like the Queen of England.

"Ready for what?" I asked.

"To give chase to the headless chicken," she replied. "It's a game all children play here."

I glanced at Pete and shrugged my shoulders. I wanted to fit in. I didn't want to be the weird boy who *wouldn't* chase a chicken.

"Sure," Pete said.

"Whichever one of you catches the chicken gets to eat the heart," she explained. "I'll fry it up in a special Bajan sauce just for you."

"Okay," I replied, thinking that we could never have played this game in Florida. Nobody killed their own chickens in Florida. People just went to the supermarket and bought those pre-killed chickens that looked as if they're made out of yellow rubber. And butchers hide the heart and innards in a little pouch tucked up their butt. Who would want to eat something that was stored there?

"Then get ready," Marlene ordered.

"Ready," I replied.

"Me, too," said Pete.

She held the chicken down with one strong black hand and raised the machete up over her head with the other. The wind picked up and her wide orange dress snapped around her like a mad flame. She looked at us. "On your mark," she hollered. We squatted down into a sprinter's pose. "Get set." She brought the machete down in a hard straight line. *Whack!* The chicken's head shot off to the side as the blade hit the wood. Quickly she picked the chicken up and set it on its feet. "Go!" she shouted.

The headless chicken dashed off. Its wings flapped, its feet clawed the air. It hopped and zigzagged in all directions. The blood shot up from the red hole in its neck like bursts of smoke from a runaway train. It ran beneath a sticker bush and we crawled under, scratching up our backs. It scampered behind a pile of bricks. We followed. It suddenly turned around and flew right at us.

"Arghhh," Pete shouted, covering his face with his hands.

A big hot splash of blood shot out of its neck and hit me in the eyes. I stuck out my arms and blindly snatched the chicken out of the air. I held the headless chicken up over my head. "I won! I won!" I shouted. Blood dripped from its neck and ran down the inside of my arm.

Pete crawled out from under a bush. He had a fresh clot of blood stuck to his forehead and he looked as if he'd been shot between the eyes.

"Let's do it again," he shouted.

But the chicken was out of steam. When I set it back down on its feet, it fell over like a windup toy that had wound down.

"It's drained," Marlene said. "Finished." She should know. She was the chicken expert.

Suddenly the back door to the kitchen flew open and Betsy stepped forward and stood on the landing with her hands on her hips. She was angry. "You've become a bunch of savages," she shouted. "Look at yourselves."

Marlene shrugged.

"We're just playing," I yelled back. I was covered with chicken blood. It was drying on my clothes in crusty brown-and-red patches. It was matting up in my hair. It was smeared across my face and under my fingernails.

"Well, you should read *Lord of the Flies*," she said smugly. "*Then* you'll see what happens to people who are stranded on tropical islands."

"We're *not* stranded," I shouted, and wiped my bloody hands on the back pockets of my pants.

"As far as I'm concerned, we're stranded," she said.

It had been two months and she was still mad because we had moved to Barbados from Fort Lauderdale. She complained that we had left *civilization* behind. I would never call Florida civilized. People might dress fancier in Florida, or drive new cars, but every time you picked up the newspaper they were shooting each other over money and drugs. People here didn't have a lot of money, but they were nice. To me, that is what civilization is all about.

Then she pointed at Pete. "You, come with me," she ordered. "You look like a cannibal."

He had wiped his bloody hand across his mouth and did look like he had eaten a hunk of raw flesh. "Don't go," I said.

"Don't listen to him," Betsy insisted. "He only gets you into trouble."

Pete looked at her, then at me. "Come on," he said to me. "We have another chicken to catch."

Yes! I thought. Pete is on my side. He is under my control.

"You're making a big mistake," Betsy warned him. "If you listen to Jack, bad things will happen to you."

"Don't listen to her, Pete," I whispered. "The heat has gone to her head and she's miserable because she can't find any friends."

"Don't say I didn't warn you," she shouted to Pete.

"When you see what Jack turns into, you'll come running back to me. Hopefully, it won't be too late to save you." She stepped inside and slammed the door.

He'll never come running back to you, I thought. Pete is mine.

"Are you ready?" Marlene asked. She had the second chicken held down on the stump and it was squirming.

"Ready," Pete replied and puffed out his chest.

Whack! Marlene chopped off the head. I snatched it in midair and stuck it onto my fingertip as the beak opened and closed without a sound. Marlene set the chicken on the ground.

"Go," she hollered.

I let Pete get a head start. I figured it was good to let him catch the chicken, since he had just listened to me over Betsy. It was his reward. But I made him earn it. I pushed him out of the way, then tripped, fell, and grabbed my foot. He got up and chased the chicken around the pepper plant. Actually, my foot really hurt and I lay on my back with my foot between my hands and moaned as I rocked from side to side. It felt as if I had stepped on a long thorn. I examined the top of my foot and gently ran my hand over the skin to check if the thorn had come all the way through. It hadn't, but the pain was killing me.

Finally, the chicken ran out of blood and Pete caught it by the wing and dragged it back to Marlene.

"What's wrong with you?" he asked as he passed me.

"I must have stepped on something," I said. I stood up but put all my weight on my left foot while I managed my balance with the toes of my right foot just touching the ground.

Marlene sat down on the stump and began to yank the feathers off the chickens. "You boys better clean up or your mother will be vexed with me."

She was right. If Mom saw this much blood on us she would have a heart attack. We went to the back of the garage and turned on the hose. I sprayed Pete down and rubbed the blood off his face and arms. Then he washed me. The blood didn't come out of our shirts very well, so we hid them inside the garage. Mom had seen centipedes in there and didn't go in very often.

I hopped on one foot back around to the side of our house to my bedroom windows. I loved my bedroom. The windows were tall and had hinges on them, so that they opened out like French doors. From the lawn I stepped right into my bedroom. I liked having my own entrance. If I wanted to sneak out at night, I could just open my windows and take off.

I limped over to my bookshelf and pulled down a large volume on table manners written by Amy Vanderbilt. I gave it a shake. It rattled inside like a drawer full of silver spoons. The title was printed in gold lettering. I wondered if I could scrape the gold off and sell it. I certainly didn't want to read about table manners. I already knew them all. *Chew with your mouth closed. No burping. Say please and thank you. Don't blow your nose in your napkin.* I sat down on the floor with the book across my lap and worked off the three rubber bands which held the covers and pages together. It's not that the book was worn out from use. Someone must have given it to us as a gift, because a book on table manners is not something Mom or Dad or even Betsy would go out and buy. They all knew that even if Pete and I read the book a hundred times we'd still chew food with our mouths open, prop our elbows on the table, and burp like pig-men.

This book was my toolbox. It was hollowed out inside. I opened it up and searched through the old tools I had stored within the carved-out pages.

One day before we had left Florida to live in Barbados, Mom had come into my room with her industrial-strength vacuum cleaner.

"I have something big to tell you," she said.

I was suspicious. Any minute, I expected her to lunge at me with the vacuum nozzle and try to suck the wax out of my ears.

"We're getting ready to move two thousand miles away. Your dad got a new job in Barbados."

I already knew this. Betsy had overheard them talking at night and had told me.

"Well, I want you to know that we can't take everything we own. We all have to make some sacrifices. You can bring your clothes, your books, and your diaries. But not"—and she waved the vacuum nozzle around the room—"all this junk. Candy wrappers. Bottle caps. Insects. Newspaper clippings. And I mean it. So get rid of it, or I will."

She turned and marched out of the room, leaving the vacuum behind as a threat. The first thing I did was open the vacuum cleaner and go through the dust bag. I had hidden a few dried bugs in Betsy's room, but since Betsy hadn't screamed and come after me with a shoe, I figured Mom had found them first and sucked them up. And, sure enough, they were in the dust bag. I picked them out and blew the dust off their cracked skin. Then I slipped them into my top pocket.

Mom and I had been fighting over my junk for a long time. She thought I was too old to collect stuff that she claimed had *no meaning*. But my junk meant everything to me. We had already moved about a dozen times, and I wouldn't have any souvenirs of where I had lived, who my friends and neighbors were, and what schools I went to, unless I saved little bits and pieces of it. I had already learned how to save a lot of my flat junk by hiding it in my normal diary. I had stapled in my baseball cards, glued in my stamp collection, taped in my pennies, as well as my photograph collection, newspaper clippings, Chinese fortune-cookie fortunes, postcards, and gum wrappers. But chunky stuff, like rocks and shells and bottle caps and marbles, was difficult.

Then I had remembered a movie where a detective took a big heavy book down from a library shelf and opened it up. Inside, the book was hollow. The middle of all the pages had been carved out, which left a big hole behind. Inside the hole was a bottle of poison. I didn't have poison, but I liked the sneaky hiding place inside the book. So I went out to the living room and took a bunch of old books that nobody ever read down from a shelf. Then I went out to the garage, where Dad kept all his carpentry tools. With a wallboard knife, I cut out the middle of the pages. It was easy. Then I went back into my bedroom and began to fill the books up with all my junk.

When it came to my tool collection, I carved out the inside of the fat Amy Vanderbilt book on table manners.

When I finished, I put in my pliers, screwdriver, tack hammer, screws, nails, nuts and bolts.

That was two months ago. Now I took out the needle-nose pliers. I had to perform surgery. Whatever I had stepped on throbbed like a bad tooth. When I held a mirror up to the bottom of my foot, I saw that it wasn't a thorn or a piece of glass. It was a plantar wart about the size of a tiny cauliflower. "Wow," I said when I saw it. "Gross." I put the mirror down and touched it. "Ouch," I cried. I looked at the wart again. I couldn't believe something was growing on me, growing *in* me. What nerve. But it scared me. It was like something alien taking over my body. As though I might suddenly grow a second nose or a third ear. I couldn't let the wart take over my body. I grit my teeth and got a deep grip on it with the pointy tips of my needle-nose pliers.

"So long, Mr. Wart," I growled. "One . . . two . . . three." I squeezed down on the handles and yanked the wart straight out. I thought I heard something rip.

For an instant I felt relief, then suddenly the pain hit me like a hot needle jammed into my foot.

"Aggghhhh," I moaned and rolled over on my side. I held my breath and fought back the pain. "Mind over matter," I said to myself, and pounded the floor. "Mind over matter," I repeated. But I was losing the battle. The pain roared back and blood squirted out of the hole just like it had squirted out of the chicken necks.

I crawled over to my bed and pulled myself up by the headboard. "Oh, crap," I said. "Oh, crap." I hopped over to the door and opened it. I peeked down the hall. Betsy had her door closed, and no one else was in sight. I hopped on my good foot and leaned against the wall. Every now and then my hurt foot touched the floor and I nearly hit the roof.

When I got to the bathroom I locked the door. I held my foot over the bathtub spigot and turned on the water. "Aggghhh." It burned.

When the blood slowed, I wrapped the hole with gauze from the first-aid kit and taped it up.

Suddenly I heard Betsy shout. "What's this blood in the hall?" She pounded on the bathroom door. "Open up!" She tried the knob. "You know you're not allowed to lock the door." She pounded on it again. "Is this chicken blood?"

"No," I shouted, and hurried to wipe up the blood in the tub with toilet paper and flush it down the commode.

"Mom!" she hollered. "Mom! Come here."

Then Mom was pounding on the door. "What's all this blood?" she asked.

Now Betsy's done it, I thought. I took a deep breath and opened the door. "I only yanked a wart out of my foot," I said casually. "I just put on a bandage. It's no big deal."

"You're more disgusting than I thought," Betsy said and twisted up her face into a warty shape.

"Did you clean it out well?" Mom asked.

"Yes," I replied.

"Did you use peroxide?" she asked.

"Yes," I said, lying.

"Okay, then. Just clean up the hall."

"Disinfect it," Betsy added. "Use hot water. I don't want any voodoo wart seeds getting on my feet."

"There is no such thing as a wart seed," I said.

"Just look in the mirror," she cracked back.

"Enough," Mom ordered. "Jack, clean the hall."

"Okay," I moaned, and hopped away like a lame rabbit.

That night my foot was killing me. I sat on my bed with a penknife and carved a little hole into the cover of my diary. When it was big enough, I removed a wad of tissue from my shirt pocket. I unwrapped the tissue and inspected the wart. I didn't want to touch it, because of the wart-seed idea. I didn't want a family of warts growing on my fingertips. I jabbed at the wart with the point of my knife, then pressed it into the hole with the handle. Just to be on the safe side, I stuck a piece of clear tape over its bumpy surface. It looked like something dead in a glass coffin. "Rest in peace," I whispered.

I opened my diary and drew a rough map of our neighborhood over both pages. I wanted to make a list of all the people who might be my friend. I didn't want Betsy to beat me at making new friends. She was always boasting that she was more popular than I was, because I was *clueless* on how to be a friend. But I knew more than she thought I did. Dad had taught me the rules. Being a good friend meant you were a good listener, always told the truth about what you liked and disliked, and tried to lead by example, not by threats. And you had to know how to tell good jokes and stories. I knew he meant that telling good jokes and stories was the most important part. The other stuff he just said because it was his job to sound like a parent.

I wanted to sneak up and down the street and locate the neighbors' names so I could write them on my map. But my foot hurt too much to creep around. I limped over to my French doors and stepped outside. I climbed the avocado tree until I was high enough to see down the street. I had my diary with me. It was dark and there were no streetlights. Each house looked like a ship out on the ocean. I could only spot the houses by the light in their windows. Actually, I could hear more than I could see. It was so quiet that I heard a boy at one house ask his mother if he could have a bowl of ice cream. She said no. I wrote "no ice cream house" down on my map of the neighborhood. I didn't know their names yet, but I knew I wouldn't be going there for dessert.

Every time I needed to write something down, I had to strike a kitchen match and hold it with my left hand while I wrote with my right hand. When my fingertips started to get hot, I dropped the match inside the diary and smothered it.

I watched a car turn the corner. It passed our house and stopped three houses down. A huge family piled out. They spoke loud but I couldn't understand them. It sounded like Arabic. My grandfather was from Lebanon. He'd died before I was born, but Dad sometimes recited poems in Arabic, so I knew how their talk sounded.

Once the car doors closed, it was pitch-black. They all went inside their house, and room by room, lights appeared in the windows. I struck a match to make a note on my map. "Arabs," I wrote.

For a long time, nothing happened. From staring out into the shifting darkness I got drowsy. I didn't want to fall asleep and pitch headfirst out of the tree and snap my neck.

I had had enough pain for one day. I climbed down and went to bed.

Three days later I woke up speckled with boils and blisters.

"Ahhhg!" I cried out in a panic. "Help! I'm sick! I'm dying!"

I went running to Mom. "Oh my God," she said, horrified. Then she hollered for Dad. "Jack!" she yelled. "Come here quick!"

Dad took one look at me, made a disgusted face, and grabbed his car keys. Mom ordered me to get dressed and ran to her room. As I was putting on some clothes, I heard her talking to a receptionist at Bayley Clinic. "It's an emergency," she said. "We'll be right over."

She was right. Dad drove like a maniac. "Move it, you slugs!" he kept shouting out of the window. He honked the horn the entire time, madly waved his fist, and nearly flattened a dozen people on bicycles.

The building was like Dr. Frankenstein's laboratory. A nurse and a doctor were waiting for us. They rushed me into an examination room and told Mom and Dad to wait in the hall. The nurse made me lie down on a bed while the doctor injected a needle into my sores and withdrew samples of the pus and blood. He seemed very serious. "Did you eat anything unusual?" he asked and poked at my draining sores with a cotton swab.

"No," I replied.

"Any bug bites?"

"No."

"Any plant allergies?"

"No." He didn't ask about warts and I didn't volunteer anything.

At the end of the examination he told me to stand up and then he escorted me to the waiting room. I put a big smile on my face to keep Mom and Dad from going crazy. But inside I was full of fear. Maybe Betsy was right and I had some voodoo chicken plague.

"I'll call you tomorrow," he said calmly to Mom and Dad. "I'll have some blood results by then."

That night I heard my parents talking about me. They were standing toe to toe in the dining room.

"I want to go home," Mom said. "The nurse said it might be leukemia."

"What does she know?" Dad said. "If it was leukemia, the doctor would have said something."

"Well, I'd feel better if we were back in Florida."

"Forget Florida," Dad said. "We're living in paradise."

"It's not paradise if you die here."

"Don't get carried away. He'll be fine. Let's just see what the tests show before we get too worked up."

"I don't want to take a chance on his health."

"We're not taking chances. You're getting hysterical."

Mom's voice rose a full octave. "Hysterical!" she screeched. "If the test results are bad, we're leaving."

I didn't want them to catch me spying, so I hopped down the hall on my good foot. Now I've done it, I thought. I've ruined paradise.

The next day the doctor called us back to the clinic. Mom asked him if I had leukemia.

He smiled. "No. It's just simple blood poisoning."

Then he turned and stared directly at me. I felt my heart racing. I thought of that little chicken just before Marlene had lowered the machete. *Whack!* And then she'd cooked him.

"Did you step on anything rusty?" he asked.

Mom's eyes widened. "You did tell him about your wart, didn't you?"

"No," I said to her. She rolled her eyes. Then I faced the doctor. "I pulled a wart out of the bottom of my foot with a pair of pliers."

The doctor leaned forward and placed his hand on my forehead. He must have thought I had a fever and was talking nonsense.

I looked over at Mom. She hunched down in her seat and covered her eyes with her hand.

"May I see your foot?" the doctor asked.

I pulled off my shoe, then my sock. He unwrapped the gauze bandage. "It doesn't hurt so much anymore," I said.

He poked at it. "It looks a bit angry," he replied. "How clean were the pliers?"

"I found them on the street," I said. "They were a little rusty." I turned to Mom. She was staring at me in disbelief.

"Well, that would explain it. What you need are antibiotics for the infection and Gentian Violet for the boils."

In a minute the nurse arrived with a big purple bottle. "Please remove all of your clothing," she said. She unscrewed the cap and poured the medicine into a shallow bowl. Then she put on a pair of rubber gloves and dipped balls of cotton into the medicine.

I took off my clothes and watched as she painted me purple from head to toe. Mom stood to one side and smiled.

Betsy and Pete ganged up on me. Every chance they had, they made fun of me. Two days later, Mom had to reapply a fresh coat of purple paint. When I slinked out onto the breakfast porch Dad took pity on me.

"You've got a choice, purple boy," he said and rubbed the top of my head. "Either we can go to the kennel and get a dog, or I can take you to the carnival."

That was an easy decision. "Carnival," I replied.

"Good choice," Betsy mumbled. "There's no reason to scare *man's best friend* to death."

"Give him a break," Dad said. "It's not easy being purple."

"It's not easy being seen with him either," she replied.

"I'll be ready in a few minutes," I said. I retreated to my bedroom. Earlier I had carved a foot-shaped pad of foam rubber out of my bed pillow. I taped it into my sneaker and tried it on. When I walked a little on the side of my foot, it didn't hurt at all. Okay, I said to myself. I'm making a comeback. Maybe I'll find a friend at the carnival.

At the carnival we played some skill games. We threw hoops over bottles and shot at ducks and tested our strength. I didn't win anything.

"Too bad they don't have a chicken-chasing contest," Betsy said when Dad stepped away to speak with a man who was working with him on the hotel renovation. "You might win a stuffed wart."

I glared at her.

Just then a booming voice came out of the overhead loudspeaker. "Ladies and gentlemen, come into the Egyptian tent and see one of the seven wonders of the natural world. Come see and hear the incredible life of the Alligator Lady. She walks! She talks! She crawls on her belly like a slime-y rep-i-tile!"

"Let's go there," I said.

"I have a better idea," Betsy said. "Let's put a tent around you . . . 'He's poxed! He's purple! He chases headless chickens like the purple freak he is!' "

"Come on, Pete," I said. "Let's play some games."

"Forget it," he replied and wrinkled up his face at me. He was definitely out of my control. Betsy had won him over.

"You'll be sorry you betrayed me," I said. "Betsy will turn you into a priss."

"Come on," Betsy said and grabbed Pete's arm. "Let's go look at the baby goats. They're so *cute*."

"See what I mean," I said.

I waited until they were out of sight. Then I went to the baseball throw. The man running the booth eyed me suspiciously. I bet he wanted me to wear gloves. For some stupid reason I had tears in my eyes, and when I threw at the bottles, I couldn't hit a thing. The first two balls missed by a mile. I threw the third so wide of the mark I hit the operator's coffee cup. It flew off the table and smashed against a chair leg.

"Hey!" he said. "You're going to have to pay for that."

"You'll have to touch me first," I shot back, then turned and ran. Being disgusting was good for something. I dodged a bunch of people as I cut down the path past the

game booths. Everywhere, there were painted signs and
posters of silly clowns and goony animals with crossed eyes
and crazy costumes. I must have looked like one of them
that came to life. A kind of diseased Pinocchio, I thought. I
kept running and people kept stepping out of my way. I
passed the bumper cars, the Ferris wheel, the spinning
teacups, the centrifugal force machine. I felt like I could run
forever. My foot didn't hurt at all. I wanted to run home. I
just didn't know the way.

When I slowed down I didn't see anyone from my family. I spotted the Alligator Lady tent and walked over to get
a closer look. They charged a dollar, so I paid up and went
in. It was dark and I didn't seem so purple. Egyptian flute
music was playing from a tinny speaker. There was a little
stage with a grassy curtain and papier-mâché palm trees. In
front of the stage, men were lined up about three deep. It
was hot and smelly under the tent, like a swamp. A barker
in a dirty white suit and pith helmet was explaining that the
Alligator Lady was netted by Egyptian fishermen on the
Nile. "She's the cousin of mermaids . . . She is over a thousand years old and has seen her husband killed by
Napoleon's troops and turned into riding boots."

The music speeded up. The curtain lifted and a large
woman in a reptile suit crawled out. I could see where the
zipper had split down the side of her costume. She must
have gained a little weight. A long alligator mask was
strapped to her face with thick green elastic straps. They
tried to disguise the phony suit by sticking a lot of slimy
leaves and pond scum all over her.

She crawled across the stage on her belly like someone

crawling under her bed. She peered up at the circus barker and hissed.

"She's a fake," a man said.

No kidding, I thought.

At first I felt cheated when I saw she was a fake, but then I didn't mind. I really felt sorry for whoever was in that costume. I should be her friend, I thought. I could run away and join the circus and live with the freaks and they would accept me as the purple boy and be my friends.

"You can ask her questions," the man in the white suit said. "She can predict the future."

"When do I get my dollar back?" asked a wise guy.

The Alligator Lady cocked her head and turned to glare at the man. "Listen," she said in an irritated tone. "I'm hot and sweaty and this is the only job I could get, so give me a break."

Everyone took a step back.

"Hey honey, don't bite," the wise guy said.

The man in the white suit waved his cane over his head. "She is not feeling well today," he said. "Her malaria is acting up."

I wasn't feeling well either. Suddenly I thought I might vomit. I didn't want to throw up and steal the show. I turned and went back outside. The light was so bright my head hurt. Maybe I have a headache, I thought, though I wasn't sure what a headache was supposed to feel like. In the movies, when people had headaches, they went to bed or fainted. When Mom had one, she seemed grouchy. When Betsy had one, she didn't want to do anything but pout.

My eyes hurt. Maybe I don't have a headache, I thought. Maybe I really am sick. Maybe I have a deadly disease and no one has the guts to tell me. Maybe Dad brought me to the carnival for one last good time before I croak.

"Hey, purple chicken eater," Pete said, sneaking up behind me. "Where've you been?"

"None of your business, Betsy's pet," I replied.

He stuck out his tongue. "Look what I won." He held up a stuffed red devil.

"I bet Dad won that for you," I said.

"Betsy did." He frowned. "What's wrong?"

"Headache," I said and shielded my eyes from the sun. "I need to lie down."

That night my foot felt better. It was still sore if I stepped hard on the wart hole, but if I wanted to make friends before Betsy, I had to get going. She was already starting to plant flowers in the front yard, and it wouldn't take long before a neighbor stopped by to introduce herself. Betsy'd pounce on her like a cat. I'd never hear the end of her calling me a "friendless purple freak."

I got my diary and map and opened my French doors. In the darkness no one could tell I was purple. I removed a kitchen match from my pocket and stooped down to scratch it across the asphalt. It snapped to life. I shielded the flame behind my diary and walked a little ways until I came to a driveway. My match went out and I stood still until my eyes adjusted to the dark. When I looked around, I saw the faint outline of a white mailbox. I leaned toward it and struck another match. NAIME was painted in big red block letters. It was the Arabs' house. I dropped down to my knees, opened my diary, and wrote NAIME on my street map. One down, I thought. I jogged for a little bit, until I thought I must be close to another mailbox. I stooped down and struck another match. There it was. HUNT. I wrote that down on my map. The next house was easy because their porch light was on. GRANTHAM. Then there was a lot of darkness. I jogged for a little distance and lit another match. Nothing. I jogged some more. The road curved to my right and I kept jogging. It felt good to run a bit. I wanted to get my health back.

I stopped and lit another match. I found a driveway, or was it a road that took a left turn? I couldn't tell. I didn't see a mailbox, so I jogged a little ways farther. I lit another match and found I was standing next to a bicycle that was propped against the front porch stairs of a big house. I dropped the match and stepped on it as I crept back out of the driveway before someone threw a net over me. I crossed the street and checked for mailboxes on the other side of the road. I lit a match and just then heard footsteps.

"Hey!" a boy hollered. "Hey!"

I threw the match down and started to run. I figured I was going in the right direction.

"Hey!" he said. "Stop."

I picked up my pace.

He picked up his pace.

I turned it on. My foot throbbed, but I wanted to get home. I didn't want someone to catch me snooping around. They might think I was a burglar and I'd get a bad reputation and never make a friend.

"Hey," he shouted. He was gaining on me. "Slow down."

I speeded up. If my foot wasn't so tender I could take off and leave him in the dark.

He speeded up.

I turned it on even more.

The steps kept coming. They were right behind me.

"Hey. Hey, you." He reached out and tapped me on the back.

I kept running.

"Hey," he said. "Slow down."

I was doing that anyway. My lungs felt like they were being ripped out of my chest. My feet slapped at the tar as I slowed down. My foot throbbed.

He slowed down, too.

I put my hands on my hips and walked in a wide circle. He did the same.

"Are you new?" he asked between breaths.

"Yes," I huffed. Even though it was dark I covered my purple face with my hands and diary. I stared out at him. He was only a slightly darker shadow against the night.

"Where do you live?" he asked.

I paused. The houses didn't have street numbers, just names. Dad had painted HENRY on a piece of wood and wired it to the front gate.

"Henry," I replied.

"So, you're the new kid," he said. "I heard a new American family had moved in."

"Yep," I said. "That's us."

He must have stuck out his hand to shake mine, but because it was so dark, he kind of poked me in the stomach.

I jumped back.

"Sorry," he said. "My name is Shiva."

"Jack," I replied, thinking that Shiva was an odd name for someone with an English accent. I stuck out my hand and searched for his as if I was reaching for a doorknob in the dark.

"Do you want to join our track club?" he asked.

I did, but I said, "Not just yet. I need to practice some more." No club would have me until I got rid of this purple stuff first.

"Well, I'll pass by sometime and we can run," he said.

"I only run at night," I said. "It's cooler."

"Me too," he said. "But presently I must return home."

"Okay," I said. "I'll see you tomorrow night."

"Yes," he replied, "and I will look into what you need to join the club." Then I heard his footsteps running off behind me.

I went directly home. My heart was pounding. I had a friend hooked, but could I reel him in? Or would I lose him once he saw me in the light of day? But for now I didn't have to worry. We could run at night.

The next morning, after breakfast, Betsy was back out in the front yard planting marigolds. She had a pitcher of iced tea and two extra glasses. She was waiting for anyone her age to walk by so she could offer them a drink. She was going to beat me at making new friends. Since it was daytime, I figured my strategy was to keep her from getting a friend, instead of me finding one.

I ran back inside my bedroom and got my medicine. I put on a white T-shirt and wrote BETSY'S BROTHER in Gentian Violet across the front. Then I dabbed more on my face. I went out to the front porch and took a seat next to her table with the iced tea. She was working with her face to the street, so she didn't see me. She could plant marigolds all day and no one would stop to talk once they saw me sitting up there like a purple freak. They certainly wouldn't want any iced tea if they thought I'd drunk out of the same pitcher.

A car drove by. I stood up and pointed to my shirt. The driver smiled and waved to me. God, I thought, people here are so nice I can't scare them away.

A second car rolled down the road. Once again, I stood up and pointed to my shirt. The driver slowed down and turned into our driveway. Betsy straightened up and rubbed her hands together to shake off the garden soil. She figured she had nabbed a victim. I smiled a great big goony smile, crossed my eyes, and waved my hands over my head. I stuck out my tongue and pushed my finger halfway up my nose.

The back door opened and a boy about my age got out. He wore a bright green silk jacket down to his knees. It sparkled under the sun. On his head he wore a silk hat the shape of an upside-down rowboat. He waved to Betsy and asked her a question. She turned and I could tell that she was surprised to see me standing on the porch. Just the way her eyes narrowed and her fists clenched told me she was furious. Pete must have heard the car. He came running out. When he read my shirt he started to laugh.

The boy waved to me. I gave him a wave back and then it struck me that he was the kid I had talked to in the dark. And I was purple. The full sun was directly above us in the blue sky and I was bright purple. I glowed like a neon sign.

He walked up the front steps and stared at me for a moment. I wiped my hands on the back of my pants.

He stuck out his hand to shake, and I did.

"You are purple," he said quietly. "Purple is a very distinguished color."

His face was the color of clay pots. His hair was jet-black. His lips were pink. "You're . . ."

"From Pakistan," he said, helping me out.

"This is my brother, Pete," I said. "He's not purple, but we like him anyway."

Shiva smiled. He opened his jacket and removed a pamphlet from the inside pocket. "I wanted to give you the information on the track club," he said.

I took it from him and set it on the table with the iced tea. My hands were sweaty and I left purple fingerprints on the paper. "I think," I said slowly, "that it would be best if I joined after I got over this purple problem."

"Perhaps, yes," he said. "I understand. Although it is a very nice shade of purple."

I was certain he was the most polite person I had ever met, and I desperately wanted him to be my friend. "But we can still run at night," I suggested. "My foot was hurting me, but it's gotten better."

"Very good," he said. "I will see you tonight. For now, I have to go." He turned and nodded toward the car. His father waved at me. All of his teeth were gold. I waved back.

"Come by after sundown," I said. "Knock on the French doors on the side of the house." I pointed to where they were.

"Very good," he replied, and nodded. He walked

quickly down the stairs. He said something polite to Betsy, then got back into his car.

As they backed out of the driveway Betsy marched toward me.

Pete tugged on my hand. "Can I run with you?"

"Forget it, traitor," I replied. "You can stay home and plant marigolds with your new friend."

Before Betsy could reach me I pulled the shirt up over my head. "I won't be needing this anymore," I said to her.

As she tramped past, she grumbled, "You'll always be a freak to me."

I threw my shirt into the front yard. "That's why I have friends," I replied.

Naime told me that if you ca...
initials on a rubber
and bury

leaf
n
dirt
days
up and
ots then
ve will
so I did it.
spot every day.
day I dug it
rotted from
I felt like a jerk. So I carved
Naime's name and Betsy's on a l...
buried that. Hopefully a rubber

on a rubber
and bury
and
later you d
if it has g
the person
love you ba
I watered t
after the se
up. It ha
all my wa

J. + H.
A.   P.

Love

*B*etsy pounded on my bedroom door and desperately rattled the knob back and forth. "Open up!" she hollered. "Unlock the door! Hurry!"

Something in her voice scared me. I dropped my book, leapt at the door, and turned the key. She pushed the door into my toe and I staggered back a step and bit my lip.

"Mom and Dad and the Pinks have been lost at sea," she cried out. "The *Privateer* was caught in a storm and went down somewhere off of Saint Lucia."

I froze. For a moment I didn't know if she was trying to trick me into dropping to my knees and crying out loud. She was still mad at me because I had taken the pins out of her door hinges, and the last time she slammed her door in my face, it fell off. I knew she must have been thinking of a way to get back at me. Seeing me drop to my knees in total despair was her idea of a good time.

"How do you know they're lost?"

"Mr. Steamer told me," she replied. "He just called from the Aquatic Club. He heard it over the shortwave radio."

"Have they drowned?" I asked. "They must have lifeboats."

"Idiot," Betsy said. "They were in a storm. If their sixty-foot yacht sank, then they won't survive on an eight-foot dinghy." Then she burst into tears.

"Are you sure you're not kidding me?"

"I wouldn't joke about them dying!"

"I'm sorry," I said as tears filled my eyes. "I don't mean to be such an idiot."

"I'm not upset with *you*." She sobbed. "You may not always be an idiot, but they'll always be dead. Now I have to tell Pete . . . and the baby."

Just then the phone rang. Betsy dashed off to pick it up. I ran right behind her. "Yes?" she said gravely. Then she let out a great sigh of relief. "Oh, that's great. Thank God. When do you think they'll arrive? Okay. Thank you for calling."

She hung up and turned to me. "They didn't sink," she said and wiped her eyes on her shirt sleeve. "A British Navy cutter got their SOS and rescued them, and the yacht. They should make it to Bridgetown this evening."

"That's great," I said and slumped back against the wall.

We were quiet for a minute, until Betsy said, "Jack, I was wrong about a couple things. Mom and Dad aren't dead, and you will always be an idiot."

She turned and went back into her room. Our one moment of getting along was over. I returned to writing in my diary. Dad had told me a lesson story about one of his workers not paying attention to what he was doing when he poured hot tar down his own boot. The lesson was to pay attention to what you are doing at *all* times. I was adding it to the section under DAD HORROR STORIES.

Mom and Dad had joined the Barbados–to–Saint Lucia yacht race by being friends with the Pink family. They were so wealthy they didn't have to work. They just sailed around the Caribbean from island to island, visiting friends, attending parties, and joining fancy yacht races. Both Mom and Dad were fascinated with them. The Pinks were charming, clever, and fun to be around. And stinking, filthy rich.

What made them interesting to me was their daughter, Anne. She lived with them on the yacht. Her parents taught her all her school lessons and she got to do everything they did. And since they sailed around all day and lived in their bathing suits, I envied her. It was the perfect life.

I had memorized everything about her. She had red hair, freckles, blue eyes, pouty lips, and long arms and legs. Her favorite food was an avocado cut in half and filled with mustard vinaigrette. Her favorite book was *Island of the Blue Dolphins*. Her favorite color was periwinkle. I was madly in love with her, but it was a secret I kept to myself. Betsy had claimed Anne as her friend and I was outlawed from showing any interest in her. If Betsy found out I was in love she'd simply gang up with Dad and they'd tease me to death.

That evening we took a taxi to the harbor and waited by the Independence Bridge. Before long, the British cutter nosed around the jetty. A taut rope followed and then the *Privateer* came into view. It was sitting low in the water. There was a big wooden patch on the port side of the white bow, and a pump on deck spewed out a constant stream of seawater. I figured the yacht was balanced between sinking and staying afloat. If the pump failed they'd go down like a rock.

Mr. Pink was at the wheel. Dad was on the bow with a coil of rope. Mom and Mrs. Pink stood in the cockpit and waved. Anne was standing on the reefed boom with one leg erect and the other propped against her knee, like a flamingo. She kept her balance with one arm around the mast and the other on a wire shroud. When she spotted Betsy, she blew her a kiss. If kisses could float on air I would have stepped in front of Betsy and cupped it between my hands as if it were a butterfly.

Once the yacht was close enough, Dad jumped off and tied the bow rope around the big iron cleat on the seawall. Mrs. Pink held Mom's arm and steadied her as she staggered off the boat and onto land. Mom looked green. Her legs were still wobbly from being on the sea, and she took dizzy steps like a drunk person. Then she dropped to her knees and we surrounded her.

She held us all off with an outstretched arm while she closed her eyes and took a deep breath. I thought she was going to be seasick and we anxiously stood by. She had always had a weak stomach. But she pulled herself together and raised her head. "Come here," she said. "I thought I'd never see you all again."

We rushed forward and hugged her.

"Oh, I prayed to God to bring me home safely," she said thankfully, and took turns kissing us on the cheek.

"Where's the baby?" she asked suddenly and searched around like a frightened bird, as though the baby had fallen out of its nest and been stolen by cats. I spun around and stepped on her foot. She groaned and tipped over onto her hand.

"Sorry," I said, and made a sorry face.

"Please be careful," she begged. "I've had a rough time."

"Eric's with the sitter," Betsy replied, frowning at me. "He was sleeping when I left."

Dad strolled over. He seemed haggard but had a satisfied look on his face, as if he had just conquered a huge fear.

"How was it?" I asked. I wanted to know all the scary details. I was hoping he had a couple gruesome stories to tell me.

"Man against the sea," he said gruffly. "And man won."

"I mean, how'd you get a hole in the boat?"

"We hit a floating coconut tree and it stove in the hull."

"Oh." I thought it might be more frightening. Maybe a giant bloodthirsty man-eating white shark had tried to bite them in two.

"I'd like to know who threw that coconut tree into the ocean," he said angrily. "Absolutely irresponsible."

I guessed that it was possible that some nut threw a tree into the ocean, hoping it would sink a boat. But it seemed more possible that it had just been washed off the shore by waves. "Could have been an accident," I ventured.

"There's no room for accidents on the ocean, son," he replied. "It's a serious world out there."

Mr. Pink called him over to help fold the jib and he sprang into action.

By then Betsy was making a big fuss over Anne. I was jealous that she was getting the real story of what had happened. Dad had only told me his side of the story. I knew there must be some secret details that only Anne knew. I drifted over to her.

"Hi," I said, and waved weakly.

Betsy glowered at me. "Don't you have something better to do than to snoop around us?"

"I guess so," I replied. But I really didn't have anything better to do than to slouch about and act like a loser. Mom was fussing with Pete. Dad was doing manly things on the boat and I knew he would tell me to stay out of the way. Betsy had clearly claimed Anne as her own. I picked up a stalk of crushed sugarcane that was lying around from a cargo barge. I flicked it end over end into the water.

"Hey!" Dad shouted and pointed down at me. "That's how boating accidents happen."

"Sorry," I yelped and turned away from him. Anne and Betsy were staring at me. Betsy whispered something to Anne. They both nodded. Then Betsy said one word so loud everyone on the dock could hear: ". . . immature!"

I leaned against the fender of a parked car as though someone had punched me in the belly. I hated that word.

At the house, Dad had built a shed the length of the back yard where he kept exotic wood imported from South America. It was expensive wood he used to panel fancy hotel rooms and he had to keep it dry and safe. The roof was made of rippled tin and the walls were made of thin wood strips that had space between them so fresh air could flow to the planks and keep them from warping under the hot roof. It had become my second home.

Since the yacht wreck a week ago, Anne had been sharing a room with Betsy. And Betsy didn't want me around the house. Before she'd let Anne out of her room, she would come out first. She patrolled the halls like a prison guard. If I even stepped out of my bedroom, Betsy wanted to know what I was up to. She especially wanted to know why I was so "immature." I couldn't even open the refrigerator and get a cold glass of water without her watching me. She suspected that I was spying on Anne. And she was right. I couldn't keep my eyes off of her. I'd sit in the living room casually reading a magazine, just waiting for her to walk by so I could raise my eyes from the pages and hope to catch her looking at me. Whenever I tried this trick it was mostly Betsy who walked by, and when my hopeful eyes met her drilling stare, she'd give me a look that was so menacing I just closed the magazine and shuffled up the hall while the word "immature" slapped me back and forth across the ears. But even from my room I could hear their laughter, so I retreated to the woodshed. If I was going to have a tortured heart, it was better to be alone.

I took my diary with me. First I made a list of all the things I should do to win her over. "Talk in complete sentences," I wrote. "Floss your teeth. Always say please and thank you. Comb your hair." Soon I got tired of thinking about me. I turned to a clean white page and wrote her name across the top. "Anne, Anne, Anne," I moaned. I wrote it one hundred times.

Our cat, Celeste, meowed as she hopped up next to me

from her hiding place below. She stretched out her long thin paws and extended her sharp claws. When she pulled her claws back she scratched a row of lines across a smooth board of purpleheart wood. The lines matched the ones I had etched with the tines of my fork across the dining-room table's veneer.

I took my penknife out and wrote "Jack Loves Anne," using the lines to measure the letters. After I had carved out all the little scraps of wood, I closed my eyes and ran my fingertips across each letter of her name. I leaned forward and smelled the purpleheart wood. The fragrance of it filled my head with a cloud of smoky sweetness, as when Marlene boiled sugarcane into molasses.

"This is what her skin must smell like," I murmured to Celeste. I pressed my cheek against the smooth, slightly dusty board. I breathed deep, then rolled my head to one side and kissed the wood.

"Jack!" Pete yelled from his bedroom window. "Time for dinner." I jerked my head up and ran my fingers through my hair. My heart pounded. Not from love, but from fear of being caught kissing a plank. If anyone, especially Betsy, or worse, Anne, had seen me, I would die. Love was not something I was prepared to share with the world. Love was a dark secret, like a ship lost undersea.

"Come on, Celeste," I said and picked her up. We rubbed noses. Then she squirmed and leapt out of my arms.

It didn't take long for Dad to zero in on my secret love ship that was lost under the sea. He shined a spotlight on it immediately after the food was served.

"Do you have a crush on Anne?" he asked directly. "Because someone has been using my Old Spice deodorant. They rubbed a new stick down to a nub in less than a week."

I blushed crimson and stared at the carrots on my plate. I couldn't look at Anne. How did he know I used his deodorant? Betsy must have tipped him off. She had been sniffing the air around me as I left the bathroom after washing my hands. I pulled my elbows close to my sides. I did smell a little spicy.

"It doesn't matter if he has a crush on Anne," Betsy said. "She likes someone else. Someone more mature."

Who? I desperately wanted to know but didn't dare ask. Whatever I did, I couldn't let anyone know I was in love. I looked at Pete. He flashed Anne a smile and coyly cocked his head to one side. Oh no, I thought. Not him too.

"I think Pete is cute," Anne said and gave him a charming smile. She was just teasing. But Pete acted like he was sprinkled with fairy dust. He grinned like a deranged pixie and slid down in his seat.

I'll crush him, I thought.

Fortunately, Mom changed the subject. "We have to go shopping tomorrow," she said to Anne. "I spoke with your mother today and she said they have the boat up in dry dock but all of your clothes and school books and . . . well, just about everything was ruined by the water. She said it will be another week by the time they patch the hole but we better get a move on in order to replace all of your things."

"May I come?" Betsy asked.

"Of course," Mom replied.

A little voice in me was crying out. Can I come? Can I come? Oh, please.

"Jack," Mom said. "You can stay home with the baby."

"Can I come?" Pete asked. Mom thought about it. "Sure," she said. "You can help us carry the bags."

After dinner Dad asked me to step outside.

"Let me give you some advice, son. Women like two kinds of men. You either have to be the totally honest, up-front kind who says exactly what is on your mind. Or you have to be the cute puppy-dog type who they want to take care of. Those are your two choices in life. Naturally, I think you should be the totally honest, up-front type, like me. The puppy-dog types get a bath once a week, some flea powder, and a pretty ribbon tied very tight around their necks, if you know what I mean." He winked.

I didn't know what he meant about the ribbon. But I knew right away that I was the puppy-dog type. I would have been in heaven if she scratched my ears, patted me on the head, and said "Good boy." I would eat dog food if she fed it to me. I knew I was lovesick, but, as they say, only her kiss will cure me.

"Thanks, Dad," I replied.

"One more thing," he added. "I'll have your mother get you your own deodorant."

I nodded and walked rapidly down the front steps and around to my French doors. I got my diary and went back around to the shed. I lay down across the planks and breathed deeply. The wood was so fragrant, like a cabinet full of spices and dried fruit. I had read about a great poet who kept rotting apples in his desk drawer. Whenever he was searching for inspiration, he would pull open the drawer, lower his nose, and breathe deeply. The smell of the sweet apples would throw him into a poetic swoon.

I took another deep breath and ran my finger over her carved name. Suddenly I was struck with poetic inspiration. I opened my diary and wrote:

LOVE
Her name is Anne
My heart
Has ears
When she speaks
Love, Love, Love
I feel
Fears, Tears, Cheers!

I practiced saying it over and over again. If I only had a chance to recite it to her, then she would understand how I felt. Poetry was very powerful. Once she heard it, I was sure she'd feel the same way, too.

I finally got my chance. Two days later I was in the shed. Rain beat heavily on the tin roof. Celeste was with me when Anne opened the door. She had been caught in the storm. Her hair was wet. Her shirt stuck to her shoulders. Her arms were covered with goose bumps.

"So this is where you hide all day long?" she asked, and hopped up on the plank next to me.

"I like it back here," I said. "It's quiet and I can think deep thoughts." I rolled my head around as though it were so filled with thoughts it was about to tip over and snap my neck.

Just then Betsy ran by. "Anne!" she shouted. "Anne!" She turned toward the shed.

Go away, I prayed. There is nobody in the shed. Go away, go away, go away . . .

"Anne!" Betsy shouted again.

I locked eyes with Anne. She held one finger up over her lips. I nodded.

Betsy turned and ran up the back steps and into the house.

Anne leaned forward and began to pet Celeste. Then she spotted where I had carved "Jack Loves Anne" on the plank.

"Did you do this?" she asked.

"Yes," I said, as though I was confessing to having done something wrong. I was deathly afraid she was going to think that carving her name in wood was immature.

"It's very nice," she said and touched it as I had.

"Would you like to see something else?" I asked. Before she could answer I pulled out my diary and opened it to the page where I had written her name one hundred times.

"You've been thinking about me," she said.

"A lot," I replied.

"I've been thinking about you, too." She reached for the neck of my shirt and pulled me toward her face.

We kissed. Our lips were slippery with the rain that kept dripping from her hair. I concentrated on not sliding off and falling forward on my face.

Kissing her was dreamy, but I had to say something romantic to her. All the kissing I had seen at the movies was followed by a beautiful thought, perfectly suited to the romantic moment. I wanted to recite my poem to her, but I couldn't remember it. I just remembered the part about "My heart has ears."

I wasn't sure what to say, so I went for another kiss while my brain frantically worked at searching for the first line of my poem. But I just couldn't remember it. So I began to think of other things to say. You are my shining star. You are everything to me. If I die tomorrow, I will not have lived in vain, because we will have kissed.

Nothing I could actually say came to mind. I held my breath each time I kissed. Finally, I was breathing like I had just run a marathon. I needed some air. It was time to take a break from kissing and talk.

I was panting and gasping for breath when I looked her in the eyes. She looked into my eyes.

"Your skin smells of wood," I blurted out.

She pulled back. "I beg your pardon?"

"Beautiful wood," I said quickly, trying to recover. But in one second something had changed. Her eyes went from soft pools of blue to narrow slits. I had blown it.

"Fragrant wood. Purpleheart wood," I murmured romantically.

"I don't get it," she said.

"I mean, you know. Nice-smelling wood."

"Betsy's searching for me," she said. Her voice was blunt. "I have to go."

"Don't leave," I pleaded, sinking to begging like a puppy with the first chance I had.

She stood up. "Betsy was right," she said to me.

"Right about what?" I asked.

"Still a little green," she replied knowingly. "Immature."

Arghh!

"Betsy said I should be with older men. Now I know why. Even after I kissed Pete he didn't say I smelled like a piece of *wood*."

"Give me a second chance," I cried out. I reached for her hand. "You smell like rose petals."

She opened her mouth and stuck her finger down her throat. "Oh, gag me," she said repulsively.

Then in one terrible moment she snatched up my diary, spun on one foot, and dashed out of the shed.

I was right behind her. "Give that back," I hollered. I grabbed at the diary, missed, slipped on the wet grass, and skidded into a bush.

She ran up the back stairs and through the door. I was doomed. That's the only reason she kissed me, I thought. Betsy must have sent her on a mission to steal my diary. It was all a trick. She never really liked me. She was toying with me.

I was crushed.

I returned to the shed, flopped on my back, and limply covered my face with my open hands. I thought I had a fever. If only Anne were my nurse, she would take care of me. I imagined I was a race-car driver who'd had a fiery crash and Anne brought me back to life. I was a wounded soldier and she applied the bandages. I was an orphan and she adopted me. I was her prize student and she kept me behind for extra assignments. I'd do special reading. She'd lean over me and breathe knowledge into my hot ears. I'd beg to do hard math problems. She'd guide the pencil with her hand on mine. Then she'd paste a big gold star on my forehead. Afterward, I'd show her my diary and she could read my poems about just how deeply I loved her.

I popped right out of my fantasy as soon as I thought about my diary. I knew that Anne and Betsy were reading it at that very moment. They were giggling and laughing at every word I wrote, especially my love poem, which I suddenly remembered.

And they both were using that awful word "immature."

For the next few days I stayed out of sight. I pretty much lived in the shack out back with Celeste. She understood me, until she got tired of me always trying to pet her, and then she turned on me and scratched me across the hand. I dabbed at the lines of blood and thought, I should tattoo "Jack Loves Anne" on my hand.

"Jack," Mom shouted from the back stairs. "Anne is leaving. Do you want to say goodbye?"

I didn't answer her. She called for me again, then went back inside.

I didn't want Anne, or anyone, to see me looking so sad. So heartbroken. Besides, I wanted her to suffer. I wanted her to feel sad that I wasn't around to wish her bon voyage. Their boat was patched up and they were leaving for Trinidad in the morning.

After Mom left, I sneaked out of the shed and dashed down the side yard to the front corner of the house. The taxi was waiting in the driveway. I didn't see anyone but the driver, and he didn't count.

I ran to the guava tree in the front yard and scrambled up the trunk. I perched like a monkey on a branch. I parted the leaves in front of my face and waited. In a moment, everyone descended the front steps and gathered around the taxi. I watched as Anne hugged Mom and Dad goodbye. Then she gave a special hug to Betsy. Then she rubbed Pete's head and leaned forward and gave him a kiss. He did a little wiggle dance, like a worm. I'd squish him later. I waited for her to search for me, to ask about me, to feel pained that I didn't show up to say goodbye. But she didn't hesitate a moment. I was the farthest thing from her mind. She opened the car door and stepped inside. Dad closed the door for her. She leaned out the window as the engine started. "So long," she said sweetly. "Thank you for everything."

"Wait!" I shouted from the tree. From my moving around, the branches rustled like a beast pushing through the brush. "Wait for me!"

Betsy, Mom, Dad, and Pete turned to look up into the tree just as I dove chest forward through the branches with one hand held over my broken heart and the other pressed against my feverish forehead.

It was a perfect swoon. I kept my eyes on her face until I hit the ground like a dud bomb. I bounced on my chest and knocked the wind out of my lungs. My wide puppy eyes were filled with dirt. I tried to say something like, You are my purpleheart, but couldn't. I was gagging for air. I reached forward with my hands and clutched at the little tufts of grass. I crawled forward, inch by inch, a wounded soldier in the battle for love.

Anne looked at me with complete astonishment. I'm certain I saw her mouth make a little circle as if she were surprised. It was the most perfectly circular circle I had ever seen made out of lips. I wanted to tell her so.

"Anne," I grunted. "Save me."

She abruptly turned her head away, gave instructions to the driver, and the car pulled out of the driveway.

Betsy walked over to me and stood above my upturned face. "You are pathetic," she said and began to laugh. Then she dropped to her knees and pressed her hands to her cheeks. "My heart has ears," she said, sighing with mock love. "What were you thinking when you wrote that?"

Suddenly I leaped forward like a frog and slapped at my legs. I had fallen on a red-ant nest and they had crawled up my pants leg.

"Pete," Dad ordered. "Get the hose and spray him down. I think he needs a cold shower."

I didn't wait for Pete. I hopped up and scampered like a lunatic down the side yard and through my French doors. I closed them behind me. As I turned, I saw it. My diary was on my bed. It was open to the page where I had written one hundred Annes in a row. She had been wearing lipstick and had kissed the page and left a moist print behind. I held it to my lips. As I kissed it, I felt the ants pinching my legs.

it out loud. "I don't like to
orders, and I don't like to give
." I rubbed my eyes and said it
. It was so powerful I got goose
mps. I rubbed my arms and it fe
se I had just rubbed aladdin's lam
t seemed to me that a new Jack can
issing out of my mouth like a rop
f smoke. a tall Jack with a dee
oice and big muscles. a Jack eve
one listened to. a Jack who could
drowning people and tell Mr. Cue
to change his name from a vegeta
to a mineral. a Jack who could
up to his Dad without having t
his undershots.

New Power

It was the middle of summer and the flies were driving us nuts. There were millions of them. We were overrun. Our house didn't have window screens, so they buzzed us all day and all night. But I had a plan. I knew that if you want to wipe out snakes you introduce the mongoose, its natural enemy, and before long the snakes are eaten and gone. If you want to get rid of mice, you buy a cat. And I knew that to get rid of flies you bring in lizards. So I did. I went out to the back yard and trapped a dozen and set them loose in my room. At first it was great. They zapped the flies with their long sticky tongues and swallowed them whole. But soon they ate so many they got fat and full and lay about the room with their eyes closed and arms and legs spread open like burned-out tourists.

I stomped around the floor with a ruler, shouting, "Wake up! Time to sing for your supper. Eat! Eat!" I slapped the ruler against the wall and startled them into moving their lizard lard. But they were useless and only lurched forward a few inches before taking another siesta.

"Forget that idea," I said out loud. "This is a man's job."

I got the flyswatter and went to work. *Whack!* One down. *Whack!* Another. Killing them properly is all in the wrist. If I swatted them with too much force, I splattered fly juice all over the wall and had to scrub them off with a rag dipped in bleach. It worked better to snap my wrist very crisply, like hitting the triangle in music class.

Whack! Whack! Whack! I became bloodthirsty. One at a time wasn't good enough. I lined up two at a time. Three at a time. I swatted them out of midair. Eventually I became so fast I grabbed them with my bare hand and held them underwater in the sink until they drowned. By the time my frenzy was over, I counted 173 dead. But it didn't make a dent in the fly population. One hundred and seventy-three flies immediately buzzed through my window and took their place. I tried to rally my lizard workers to eat more. But they were stuffed, and when I smacked the ruler around their tails they wouldn't even tremble. I accidentally hit one and cut its tail off. I picked it up and pressed the broken part against the tip of my nose. The lizard blood was thick and gummy. The tail wiggled around like a tiny bullwhip. "Mush. Mush!" I shouted and lowered my nose so the little whip lashed their backs. They didn't even twitch. They stuck to the wall like refrigerator magnets.

I collected my flies and pressed them into my diary. *Crunch!* It was like making a fly sandwich. Then I took a pen and wrote 173 on the plastic flyswatter flap. I planned to kill one million, save them for proof, and get into the *Guinness Book of World Records.*

But after a while the flies were no challenge. I had to move up. I had to find something more difficult to exterminate. I was getting older and killing flies was a kid's game. I went out to the back yard. We had an abandoned well filled with bats. The well opening was cemented over except for a hole the size of a brick. Every evening a ribbon of bats flew out of the hole to eat insects. They spread out and darted overhead, cutting the air up into little jigsaw pieces. Now *they* were difficult to hit. That was a challenge.

The only problem was that Dad had told me not to mess with them. "They are animals," he said. "You never throw rocks at animals." He told me this after he caught me whipping broken shards of bathroom tile at them. He said he was worried about me hurting the bats, but I knew it was really that he was worried about where the pieces of tile and rocks would land. There were a lot of houses around and he was touchy about breaking windows.

Johnny Naime told me that it was impossible to hit a bat with a rock. "They have built-in radar," he explained. "You can throw rocks at 'em all day and never hit them. You *can't even shoot* a bat. They move faster than bullets."

Cool, I thought. They were just the challenge I was after.

I got a yardstick and poked it down into the hole and stirred it around. I didn't hear anything. I put my eye to the hole and looked in. I was a bit afraid one of them would come shooting out and bite me on the eyeball, but I knew that was impossible. Dad said they ate only bugs and vegetables.

Just then BoBo II brushed against the back of my leg. I jumped up into the air. "God! You scared me."

Betsy had got him as a birthday gift. She named him after her other black spaniel, BoBo I. That was a mistake. BoBo I was a loser, and this one was even worse.

He rolled over and fell asleep. Something was wrong with that dog. It needed vitamins. And it smelled.

Suddenly a bat flew up out of the hole and fluttered back and forth overhead. I picked up a bunch of rocks and fired at it. I didn't even get close.

Then a stream of them came out in a steady black line. They zipped back and forth above the house eating millions of flies. "Eat more!" I shouted. "Get fat! Slow down and I'll nail you." I threw about a hundred rocks. Everything missed. They were about a million times harder to hit than flies.

As quickly as they had all come out of the hole, they returned into it, like the smoke sucking back into Aladdin's lamp. I waited a few minutes for them to settle down, then picked up a brick.

"If their radar is so good," I said to BoBo II, "then they can dodge rocks in their sleep." I dropped the brick down into the hole. Nothing happened. I chucked a few more pieces of brick into the hole.

A single bat came out of the well and dove at my head. It startled me and I yelled and tripped backward over BoBo II. My feet went up over my head and the bat zoomed in on my sneaker and bit it on the rubber tip. I didn't know what bat teeth looked like, but they went through my tennis shoe and missed my toe. If it's a vampire bat, I thought, I'm a quarter-inch from being turned into a vampire and living with Dracula for the rest of time. I had seen the movie.

I pumped my foot up and down, but I couldn't shake it off. I threw a rock up at it, but missed and hit my ankle. I picked up another rock and whipped it at the bat. I missed, but I heard the sound of breaking glass. Oh crap! I thought. What had I hit?

But I still had the bat to deal with. I used the toe of my good shoe to wedge the heel off my bat shoe. It fell to the ground, but the bat hung on. I jumped up and hobbled off to find what I broke.

It couldn't have been worse. It was Dad's office window. "*Ay, chihuahua,*" I moaned. "Now I've done it."

This was the second time I'd broken Dad's office window. The first time, I hit it with a tennis ball. I was playing by myself against the garage door when I smacked the ball right through the pane. It was an accident.

Dad gave me a warning which basically went: "If it happens again, I'm going to use my belt." He meant business.

I wanted to run but knew hiding would just make it worse. As Dad would say, "Take your punishment like a man." He was right. I couldn't act like a boy forever. I was already thirteen. I squatted down and picked up all the glass shards. When I was little, I always called broken glass "ghost's teeth." That seemed like a thousand years ago. This was just broken glass, plain and simple.

After I cleaned up, I wrote a note and taped it on his office door. I didn't tell him about the bat. One thing at a time, I cautioned myself. Then I returned to my room to wait. Maybe he would just come in and tell me one of his lesson stories. I flipped through the section of my diary where I wrote them down. There wasn't one for my particular problem.

"Once upon a time," I wrote, "there was a son who didn't listen to his father. He repeatedly screwed up. But the father was patient. And eventually the son figured out how not to get into trouble every day of the week. Eventually he thanked his father for his patience."

But that evening, when he opened my bedroom door, his belt was already off. I didn't even get a chance to explain my side of the story.

"You know the rules," he said.

"It was an accident," I replied, lowering my eyes.

"There is no such thing as an accident," he said, quoting himself. "There is right and there is wrong. There is thoughtful thinking and thoughtless thinking. Your thinking today was thoughtless and what you did was wrong. That is not an accident."

I felt trapped by his thinking. "It was an accident," I said weakly. "Don't you get it?"

"Children have accidents. Men make choices. Just do as you're told," he replied impatiently.

I put my hands out and leaned against the wall. He reached into my back pocket, removed my wallet, and flicked it onto the bed. Then he reared back and gave me five cracks in a row.

When he finished he slid the belt through the loops of his pants. It looked like a snake curling around his waist.

"You'll never grow up properly if you don't listen to me," he said, and left the room.

I pulled down my pants and sat on the cool floor. I decided I'd never let this happen again. I'd never break his window and I'd never let him hit me. I was tired of being on the bottom of the heap. I wanted some power of my own. I was sick of beating up flies, lizards, and bats. Those were kids' games, and the longer I played like a kid, the more I was treated like one, and the less power I had.

That night, when Mom and Dad came home from the Beau Brummell Club, they started arguing. I listened at my bedroom door. From the volume of their voices I could tell they were in the living room. They were arguing about the same stuff they always fought over. Mom wanted to return to Pennsylvania. She didn't like being so far away from her family.

"Nonsense," Dad replied. "If we lived back there, I'd be out in the snow framing houses for peanuts. That place is a dead end. We have no future there."

"Well, what do we have here?" she asked. "A bunch of rummy friends and no family."

He poured a drink. "We have friends," he said.

"And you are drinking too much," she added.

"Don't start that again," he snapped, and sat down heavily on the couch.

I picked up my diary and put a pen between two blank pages. It's now or never, I said to myself. I've got to fight back. If he wants me to listen to his every word, I've got to be close enough to hear them all. I took a deep breath, opened the door, and went down the hall. I stood by the dining-room table and stared at them. Dad was spread across the couch, with his head propped up on the arm. Mom was standing. Her black evening shoes dangled in her hand by their heel straps. She had a tissue in the other hand and was wiping off her red lipstick. I caught her speaking in midsentence.

". . . and I called Mother," she said, "and told her I wanted to come home for a few weeks."

"Do what you want," Dad said, and waved at a fly. "I can get along just fine without you complaining all day and night."

Then he saw me. He hopped up onto his feet and put his drink down as though he hadn't said or done anything nasty.

Just like an adult, I thought. Always trying to act innocent. They use one set of rules around us and another for themselves.

"What are you doing up?" he demanded.

Mom propped her hand on her hip.

"Writing," I replied, trying to keep my voice steady.

"Writing what?"

"In my diary," I said.

"He means *what* are you writing?" Mom said, stepping between us.

Then I unleashed the line I had been waiting to use. The one that I hoped would turn the tide and put me in control.

"I'm writing down all the things you say," I replied. I looked down at my diary and began to write his last question.

"Stop it," he ordered.

I wrote down *Stop it* in my diary.

"I think you should return to your room and read," Mom suggested, crossing her arms. I slowly wrote down what she'd said.

"Let me see what you've written," he commanded. He was angry. He picked up his drink and finished it. When he lowered his glass his eyes were red and narrow. My grandmother had once said to me, "Alcohol can turn the gentlest lamb into a lion." I believed her.

"Give me that." He held out his hand.

"No," I said. "When Mom gave me the diary she said it was mine."

He groaned and rolled his eyes. "Your mother told you that?"

"Yes."

Mom took a deep breath and let it all out slowly. "Anyway," she said to Dad, "I don't want to talk about it tonight."

Dad took a step toward me. I bit my lip. Here he comes, I thought. Don't look away. No matter what he does, don't look away. He's going to grab my diary and toss it across the room and take out his belt. But he didn't. He ran his hands through his hair, turned, and left the room.

"If I were you," Mom said once he was safely down the hall, "I wouldn't try this stunt too many times."

Why not? I thought to myself. It worked. I'll do it a hundred times in a row if I want to.

"And another thing," she said. "I don't like your attitude."

Great! I thought. I could feel the new power in me. The power to annoy her.

"I think you need to go to your room," she said.

"Fine with me," I replied. "It will give me more time to write all this down in my diary."

She groaned. I could tell she regretted getting me a diary. But it was too late to take it back.

I stood up and retreated down the hall. I was feeling very powerful as I closed and locked my bedroom door. I opened my French doors and stepped out. I climbed up into the avocado tree and looked up and down the street. I was taller than any of the houses. I was taller than Dad. "The pen is mightier than the sword," I whispered. I finally understood what that meant.

A few days later Mom opened my bedroom door and sat on the edge of my bed. She had just returned from having her hair and nails done. "I have something to tell you," she said seriously. "Sit down."

I sat next to her and sniffed the air. She smelled like hair spray and nail-polish remover and lots of gardenia perfume. I took a deep breath and held it in.

"I spoke with Grandma and have decided to go up and visit her for a month. I'm taking Pete and Eric . . . but you and Betsy have to stay here."

"Why?" I blurted. "I'm always left behind." I felt betrayed.

"Because your father and I had a talk and agreed that if we stay in Barbados longer than the summer . . . maybe for a long time . . . you will have to get ready for school here."

"But it's July," I said. *"July!"*

She paused. "You have to go to summer school," she

said. "The school system here is more advanced than in Florida. If you don't go to summer school to catch up, you'll have to repeat sixth grade."

"No way." I groaned. Florida was screwing me up again. I had told her my last school was for simpletons only, but she didn't believe me. Now she knows, and *I* have to suffer the consequences. As *usual.*

"Which means," Mom continued, "that you have to stay here with Betsy and Dad for a month. I know this is not fun, but Marlene will cook and keep your clothes clean and you are old enough to be responsible."

"I'm old enough when you want me to be responsible so you can do what you want. But I'm always *too young* when it comes to doing what I want."

"You're not a kid anymore," she said. "You are a young man. Act like one." She stood up. "I don't want to hear any back talk," she said in her bossy voice. "You understand that this is the best situation we can work out for everyone. This whole family doesn't revolve around you and your needs." She frowned, which meant she had spoken the Truth According to Mom and that was that. She left the room.

"You've just thrown me to the wolves," I shouted. "The *wolves!*"

She opened the door and smiled at me. She was so beautiful I forgot to be mad. "Your sister said the same thing," she said, and laughed. She glided toward me and gave me a big hug. "You know," she said, "I think this will give you and your dad some time together to smooth out some of your friction."

"What do you mean?" I asked. I was pretty sure our

relationship was about winning and losing, about who was the boss and who was the peon.

"You know what I mean," she said. "You're getting older and you are starting to bump heads with your dad."

I wasn't ready to discuss it, so I changed the subject. "I'll miss you," I said.

"I'll miss you more than you'll miss me," she replied, and became teary-eyed, which made me feel like a jerk for ever saying anything mean to her. Even though she was leaving me with Dad and Betsy for a month, she was my mom. It was my job to be nice to her, no matter what.

Two days later they were gone and Betsy and I were eating dinner with Dad. Marlene served a platter of flying fish and okra.

"I love this fish," I said to Marlene.

"Thank you," she said in her formal voice. When she passed me, she bent forward and whispered, "We'll have chicken hearts this week."

"Yum."

"Tomorrow," Dad started, delivering the opening word to the evening announcements, "the driver will pick you up and take you to the prep school. Marlene will have your lunches packed. After school you'll come directly home and do your studies. Marlene will have dinner for you every night at six. If I'm not home, eat without me and be in bed by nine. Any questions?"

Betsy didn't argue with him. I didn't either. I pulled my plate close to my chest, lowered my mouth, and scraped the food in.

"Look at him," Betsy said arrogantly. "He uses BoBo II's

rules of eating. First, eat everything as quickly as possible. Second, eat everything you dropped on the table or floor. Third, wash it down by slurping loudly. Fourth, nose around for more. Fifth, when there is no more, lick your lips and drift away."

I stared at Dad. If Mom were here she would ask Betsy to apologize.

Dad laughed. "You know," he said to Betsy as if I weren't present, "the best way to feed Jack would be to put a funnel in his mouth and just pour it down his throat."

Now it was her turn to laugh. Without Mom, I was a Ping-Pong ball whacked back and forth.

"May I be excused?" I asked, and was halfway out of my chair.

"Only if you'll get our fishing gear organized," Dad said. "I thought you'd like to join me."

"All right." I loved to fish.

I ran into the kitchen and called Shiva. We were supposed to go running later on.

"I'm tired, anyway," he said, after I canceled. "I'm sluggish."

"I have a cure for that. Whenever I'm sluggish, Mom always gives me prunes and warm water. I guarantee that in no time you'll be on the run."

"Really?"

"Cross my heart," I said. "You'll be running like a fiend."

"Okay," he replied. "I'll try it."

I put down the phone and headed for the garage. I got our rods, tackle boxes, net, and gaff hook, then loaded it all into the truck. I knew the routine.

When Dad arrived we drove to the St. Lawrence Gap, a stone jetty starting from the back of the St. Lawrence Hotel. It curved out into the ocean like a hundred-foot-long question mark. We carried our gear to the tip and got set up. The ocean was calm. The swells slowly brushed along the rocks and sighed as they broke across the sand.

"The first one to catch a fish gets to send the other guy to the bar to get drinks," Dad said.

"Okay." It was a fair deal. That's what I liked about fishing. It put us on equal ground. You cast out your line and the fish don't know the difference between a man and a boy.

Dad reared back and cast his chrome triple-hooked spinner. The line spun off the reel. *Plop.* It landed about fifty yards away. He let it sink down and slowly reeled it in with his thumb pressed against the spool of line to feel for bites. He was going for big bottom feeders like grouper and trigger fish.

I took a different approach. I opened my tackle box and attached a bobber to my line, then got my secret weapon, a dragonfly. I put it on the hook and gently cast it out so it floated about twenty feet from the rocks. I was after surface feeders, especially red snapper, which was my favorite. Together we stood there with our rods pressed against our bellies like two guys peeing off a dock.

Suddenly my bobber went under. I counted. One, two, three. I jerked back on the rod to set the hook, and reeled it in. The fish didn't put up much of a fight, but it was the first one caught—a bluegill about the size of my hand.

"I won," I hollered. "I'll take a Lemon Squash."

"You didn't win," he replied. "That's not a fish. That's bait."

"You didn't say how big it had to be. You just said it had to be a fish."

"Well, you cheated," he said. "Anyone can catch a fish like that. I could have just stuck the net in the water and caught one of those. Now *you* have to get the drinks."

"No way," I said. "I won. You haven't caught anything yet."

"Don't argue with me," he replied. "You cheated. Besides, I'm paying. Now fetch. I'll take a Banks in the bottle. And tell the bartender your dad wants it ice-cold."

I threw my fish back into the water and took the money from his hand. *Bully*, I thought to myself. There is no winning with someone who won't play by the rules.

By the time I returned he had seen a few of his friends and waved them over. They sat down on the rocks to shoot the breeze and I couldn't get a word in edgewise.

I recast my line and drank my soda. I should have talked Shiva into running, I thought. It would be a lot more fun than watching Dad and his pals talk. And then I remembered what I told him about the prunes. I hoped he didn't take my advice. I was sure he knew better. Everyone knew what prunes could do to you.

The next morning Betsy and I were standing at the edge of the driveway. I looked up at Dad's window. It was still broken.

"Don't you get tired of being treated like a kid?" I asked.

She frowned. "Nobody treats me like a kid."

"Well, don't you hate it when adults say things like, *Do as I say, don't do as I do.*"

"I just ignore them," she said.

"Doesn't it bug you that you never get a vote on where to live, what to eat, where to go to school, what clothes to buy?"

"What are you whining about?" she shot back. "You are always complaining about something. You are the *last* person I would want making decisions around here. If it wasn't for Dad, you'd be living in a refrigerator box and raiding garbage cans for dinner."

I could tell whose side she was on. I missed Pete already. He usually agreed with me. A month of Betsy and Dad and I'd be a nervous wreck.

We were standing at the edge of the driveway when a car raced up the street and aimed straight for us. It was a big old American car with a huge hood ornament, and as it got closer it looked like a charging rhinoceros. Betsy stood her ground, but I jumped behind a fence post as it hit the brakes and skidded to a stop.

"Get in," squeaked a little voice.

The driver was a bug-eyed maniac. He was skinny, sat on a pillow, and scratched at a bald spot on his head that looked like a rug burn. He smoked unfiltered cigarettes and had a lead foot. Betsy took the front seat and sneered at him. I climbed in the back with two boys who must have been brothers, about my age and Pete's. They were pale, sweaty, and terrified. We took off with a lurch and peeled rubber up to the corner, where he took the right-hand turn without slowing to look. The car tilted like a canoe about to flip over. I tumbled across the seat and crunched into the two boys. They both grabbed their crotches and moaned.

"Sorry," I mumbled. The car straightened out and we raced a taxi to the red light, where we came to a screeching stop. The three of us bounced off the back of the front seat and fell to the floor. When I pulled myself up I was thrown back as the light turned green and our driver floored it. Betsy had her shoes propped against the dashboard and her right hand gripped the overhead strap. Her left hand was pressed against the side of the maniac's face, so he could only see with one eye. "Slow down!" she yelled.

He laughed and speeded up, then jerked his head out the window to get a better view. The engine roared as he pulled out to pass a line of slower cars and bicycles.

I glanced at the two boys.

"Okay," the older one said to the younger. "Now's your chance. We're on a straight stretch."

The speedometer needle was up to seventy-five and we were passing everything on the road. If anyone pulled out in front of us we'd be dead meat.

When I turned back toward the boys, I was shocked. They both had their pants down and were pulling plastic bags of pee off their private parts. The bags had been held on with rubber bands. The older brother, who was next to the door, threw his out the window. He then reached for his brother's full bag. It was a delicate operation made even more difficult because the bag was so full. Before he could swing it out the window, we hit a curve at seventy and the three of us were pressed against his door with my face about an inch away from the dripping pee bag. In an instant we straightened up and he tossed the bag out the window before we took a curve on my side.

When we straightened out again, the younger one attached a fresh pee bag to his privates and yanked his pants back up. I looked at the older brother.

"He scares us so much we wet our pants," he shouted over the blast of air which was screaming through the open windows. "This is all we can do to stop it."

Just then the maniac hit the brakes and we went into a sideways skid down a dirt road. We came out of the fishtail and quickly pulled into a driveway. Overhead was a sign which read ARAWAK SUMMER CAMP.

We came to a stop inches from another car and scared the passengers into ducking down. The two boys hopped out. "See you later," I said, as we spun out in a cloud of dust and flying gravel. Up the road we pulled into another driveway. PRESENTATION YOUTH COLLEGE read the sign.

As soon as we came to a stop, Betsy reached across the dashboard and pulled the keys out of the ignition. She jumped out of her side and threw them into a field of grass.

"Hey! You can't do that," the maniac squealed. He sounded like an angry Chihuahua.

Betsy raised her fist to his chin. "I just did it," she growled. "So what are you going to do about it, you little runt?"

He turned and ran into the field. He dropped down onto his knees and scratched up the ground.

"Coward," she hollered. "It's not nice to scare kids."

"That goes double for me," I yelled.

Betsy turned around and gave me the evil eye. "Oh,

shut up," she carped. "You sound tough now, but all you did was bounce around back there like a bowl of yellow Jell-O."

She was right. I hadn't lifted a finger to help out.

"What could I have done?" I asked.

"You should have covered his eyes with your hands."

I imagined just how helpful that would have been.

We went inside and found our class assignments, which were listed according to grades. There were half a dozen other kids about my age scattered throughout my room. They weren't Americans, so I figured other countries were also dishing out crummy educations.

I took a seat next to the window so I could daydream. Suddenly a very stubby, thick man marched into the room.

"Rise and stand quiet," he ordered.

We all stood.

He set his briefcase down on the desk. "My name is Mr. Cucumber," he said as though he were angry about it. "I've been teaching for ten years. During that time I have expelled ten students. Do you know why?"

I did, but didn't dare answer.

"The first person to make fun of my name will repeat sixth grade . . . No ifs, ands, or buts. Period. You all understand?" We nodded mutely.

"Sit!" he ordered. We dropped down like sandbags.

He sat behind his desk, leaned back, and folded his hands behind his huge bald head. "Today is your last chance for a summer free from school. In my briefcase . . ." He tapped it with a long wooden pointer. *Tap. Tap. Tap.* ". . . I have exams that will measure your knowledge of English, mathematics, world history, and science. If you pass all four subjects, you don't come back until September. If you fail even one, you have me five days a week for six weeks in a row until I mash some knowledge into your empty brains."

I could not think of one fact I knew for sure about any of those subjects. I peeked at the other students. They looked as sweaty and empty-headed as me.

Mr. Cucumber stood, removed the tests, and placed one face-down on each of our desks. "You will have an hour per section," he explained, and checked his watch. "The first section is math. Go."

I turned over my exam. I was sunk right away. I didn't even get a chance to have some tiny bit of false hope. The first problem was in meters, kilometers, decimeters, grams, and liters. I skipped that problem and leafed through the entire section. It was not multiple choice. I knew right away what I'd be doing for the next six weeks. My head drooped over like a hanged man's. I asked myself, How many meters of rope does it take to make a noose?

I did all the math I could, then quit. When the hour was up, we had a ten-minute break. I ran to find Betsy.

She was at the water fountain. When she saw me she asked, "How many grams in an ounce?"

I threw up my hands.

"Looks like I'll have the house to myself while Mom's away," she said with supreme confidence.

"Hey, just wait till you get to science," I said as snottily as I could.

"Already did it," she sang. "I skipped ahead."

I felt like an idiot.

At the end of the day the tests were graded before we went home. No one in my group passed.

"If you study, study, study," said Mr. Cucumber when he called me to his desk, "you might make it."

I felt doomed.

"One final question," he asked before I left. "Is a cucumber a vegetable or a tuber or a berry?"

This had to be a trick question. I always thought it was a vegetable. "A tuber," I guessed.

"It's going to be a long summer," he replied and grinned like a rottweiler. He did not look like a vegetarian. He was definitely a meat eater.

When I went outside, Betsy was surrounded by other girls her age. They listened to every word she said. I thought they were going to drop down and kiss her feet.

I squeezed in between her fans. "Guess what," she said to me and flicked her hair back to look more glamorous. "I did so well I get to skip a grade. And you?"

I had to turn things around. I was going downhill fast. Dad was kicking my butt. Mr. Cucumber was a fiend. Betsy was an instant success at everything. And I was a loser. I really missed Pete. It was his job to be on the bottom of the barrel. Now the entire barrel was sitting on me. I couldn't get any lower.

"Don't wait for me," Betsy said as I dropped my head in shame. "I have a different ride home."

Great, I thought, as I walked around front. Leave me with the maniac. The way he drives, they'll soon be hosing my face off the front grille of a tractor-trailer.

When the midget turned into the driveway he headed

for me like a locomotive that had jumped track. The two
boys were already bouncing around in the rear like loose
packages.

I took the backseat with them and we blasted down the
driveway and ran a car off the road when we made our
first turn. He hit the gas and I thought of covering his eyes
with my hands but didn't.

Coward, I said to myself. *Wimp. Chicken. Yellow-bellied sap-
sucker!* Betsy is more of a *man* than you are.

We took a turn and nearly hit a goat. After another
dozen killer turns we got to the straightaway. The boys desperately yanked down their pants and pulled off their pee
bags.

"Give me that," I said and grabbed the dripping bag out
of the younger boy's hands. I leaned forward and poured it
over the maniac's head. He sputtered and turned around. I
was waiting for him with the second bag. *Splash!* I got him
right in the face. He hit the brakes and reached for me. We
skidded across the road, hit the curb, bounced up, and
slammed into a chain-link fence. It stopped the car like a
big steel net. The maniac screamed and hit the floor.

We bounced off the seat. "Come on, boys," I said. "Fol-
low me." We crawled out the window as a crowd gathered.
I flagged down a cab. "Get in," I said. They did, and we
got stuck in traffic and inched our way down the road
along with the other cars, donkeys, goats, and bicycles. The
boys just stared at me as if *I* were the maniac. Ingrates, I
thought to myself.

When the taxi dropped me off in front of the house, I
paid the driver with money Mom had left me, then swag-

gered up the front steps like a big man. *Don't mess with me!* I growled and pounded my chest. *I'll pour pee on your head.*

It was Sunday. With Mom gone, Dad worked seven days a week. This morning, he was running late and was trotting around his truck. A pipe was sticking out of the overhead rack. It was head-high and just a little bit longer than the truck bed. Each time Dad ran around the truck, getting tools, moving equipment, checking supplies, he ducked under the pipe. He did it without looking, as if it was something he had practiced.

I stood in the kitchen window eating toast and beamed telepathic thoughts at him. As he headed for the pipe, I thought, *Duck.* He ducked. As he came back around, I thought, *Duck.* He ducked. Suddenly he snapped his fingers and doubled back to get something he remembered. *Don't duck,* I thought.

Bonk! He hit the pipe and his feet went straight out beneath him and he landed flat on his back. I ran down the stairs and knelt over him. I slapped his cheeks back and forth. Not so hard, I warned myself, he might come to in a bad mood. He was breathing but he was out cold. A huge lump popped up on his forehead like in a cartoon. I ran into the house to get some ice. When I came out, he was sitting up with his chin on his knees. He saw me and grinned.

"Wow," he whistled and shook it off. "That was some sucker punch you hit me with."

"That wasn't me," I said, but I felt guilty for thinking, *Don't duck.*

"No kidding," he replied and hopped up onto his feet, then wiped the dirt off his pants. "You'd have to hit me a hell of a lot harder than that to get rid of your old man."

He examined himself in the side mirror and combed his hair. He removed his handkerchief and wiped a smudge off his lump.

"See you later," he said, ducking under the pipe and opening the driver's side door. "Don't forget to give BoBo II a flea bath. He smells."

He pulled away and I strolled around to the front yard. BoBo II wasn't under the shade tree. "BoBo the Second!" I yelled down the street.

I heard him barking over by Hal Hunt's garage. I walked over there. Hal had BoBo II trapped in a corner and was throwing bullets at him. He had a box of shells in his hand, and every time he threw one, he jumped up into the air as if the bullet were going to fire and he could skip over it. "Dumb smelly dog," Hal shouted and threw another bullet. BoBo II looked puzzled. He needed a nap. He was only good for about an hour of energy each day, and his time had expired.

"Hey, what are you doing?" I hollered.

He whipped around and raised his arm over his head. "Watch it, Henry," he growled. "I've got a bullet in my hand."

"*You* watch it," I growled back. "With the power of my mind, I can make that bullet explode between your fingers." I squinted and touched my fingertips to my forehead. I stared at the bullet and concentrated.

Hal looked at me. I could tell that he wasn't certain if I was bluffing. I wasn't sure either. But I had just knocked

Dad cold, so I figured I could set off a bullet. I narrowed my eyes and concentrated so hard I moaned. My muscles knotted up and I began to tremble.

Suddenly he twisted away from my paralyzing mental grip and threw the bullet into the bushes. "You must be a devil," he cried out and stared into his hand.

"Don't mess with me," I said, lowering my hands. "I know where you live and my power is strong enough to cross the street. I can just *look* at your house and make pictures fall off the walls." Then I turned to BoBo II. "Come on, smelly," I said. He followed dutifully.

When Dad came home, Betsy and I sat down to dinner. Marlene served fried chicken, white rice, and spinach. When she left the room, Dad said, "This food is too bland." He got up and went into the kitchen and returned with a bowl of tiny red peppers. "This will fix it up," he said. He put a pepper on his plate and passed me the bowl. "Try one."

"I don't think so," I replied.

"You're chicken," he said. He hooked his thumbs under his armpits and flapped his elbows up and down. "*Bluck, bluck . . . bluck bluck*," he squawked. "Chicken."

I hated that. I looked at Betsy.

"Chicken," she said.

"I am not," I shot back and put a pepper on my plate. "Anything you can do, I can do, too."

He grinned. "We'll see about that," he said and bit his in half. "Chew it up good," he instructed and chewed with his mouth open to show me.

I took a bite. My tongue turned into a lava flow of pain.

"Grind the seeds between your teeth," he said.

I did. The pain increased, but I didn't twitch.

He finished the remainder of his pepper.

I finished mine. So this is what it's all about, I thought. Me and Dad. One-on-one. Pepper-to-pepper. This is what Mom meant when she said her leaving would give me and Dad some time to work out the friction between us. But we weren't going to be equals. One of us was going to end up on top and the other on the bottom.

"Another," he said.

I took two and chewed them up. The heat spread to my lips and curled violently up into my nose. It was like sniffing battery acid. My eyes watered but my face was so hot the tears probably evaporated.

Dad took two and chewed them. He cracked his knuckles, then settled down and took a bite of chicken. Finally, it was time to eat dinner.

I took a bite of chicken and snorted loudly through my nose. Eating food was like throwing coal into a furnace. Flames shot out my mouth, nose, eyes, and ears.

Betsy laughed. "Your hair is curling," she cracked.

"Can't take it, can ya?" Dad asked. "Can't keep up with your old man? You think you can. But you can't."

I closed my eyes and concentrated. Don't give in, I thought. Don't.

"I'll give you a hint," Dad said. "H . . . 2 . . . O."

I only had milk. "Excuse me," I whispered. I stood up and went to the kitchen. Once I was out of sight I rolled my head from side to side and let out a silent scream. My breath almost set the curtains on fire. I dove for the sink and stuck my mouth under the spigot and turned the handle. Oh my God! It was like throwing gasoline on a fire. I yanked my mouth away and almost knocked out my teeth.

I could hear Dad howling with laughter. "Water makes it hotter," he sang. "Try a piece of bread."

When I returned to the table he was still snickering. I just kept my eyes glued to the lump on his head.

"You've got to get up a lot earlier in the morning to beat me, kiddo," he said.

I took a bite of rice. It tasted like ashes.

The next morning I was standing on the street corner. Since I no longer was driven to school by the maniac, I had to take the bus. I squinted up at the sun to try and tell what time it was. I couldn't. It seemed like I had been waiting for a long time, and I didn't want to be late. Mr. Cucumber was a force to be reckoned with and I wasn't feeling very chipper. After dinner it had taken a long time for my stomach to cool down. I had spent half the night tossing and turning in bed.

"I need a watch," I said. No sooner had I said it than I spotted one lying on the side of the road. It was tilted at just the right angle, so that the sun bounced off the crystal and hit me in the eye. "Seek and ye shall find," I said. I was definitely becoming more powerful. Nothing could stand in my way. The pepper contest with Dad was just a little setback.

I picked the watch up and put it on. It was even set at the right time. I snapped my fingers. "Bus, arrive!" I shouted. In a second, the bus turned the corner and stopped in front of me. Not a bad beginning to a new day, I thought. I needed a boost.

After about an hour of Mr. Cucumber telling us how useless we were, my attention wandered to my new watch. Since I was sitting near the window, I moved my wrist so that the sun hit the crystal. I followed the angle and spotted a little patch of bright light on the far wall. Mr. Cucumber drifted in my direction, so I gazed up at him as though I were really listening. When he turned away, I adjusted the crystal so that I shot a sharp laser beam of light into the corner of his eye. With each blast I gave him, I concentrated on two words, *migraine headache*.

I had zapped him a couple good ones when he suddenly whipped around and aimed his pointer at my nose. "Do you think I'm an idiot?" he shouted, and bore down on me. He drove the pointer into my chest like a short, fat, bald, cucumber Musketeer.

I was struck dumb.

"Take the stick," he commanded. His face was as tough and scuffed up as the toe of an old shoe. "Take it!"

I pulled it away from my chest.

"Give me your wrist!"

I held it out to him.

He unlatched the watch and set it down on my desk. "Stand up!"

I stood.

"Lash it!" he shouted.

"What?" I asked meekly.

"The watch. Lash it!"

Well, easy come, easy go, I thought. I brought the stick down and hit it squarely. Nothing broke.

"Again! Harder!"

I hit it again. And again. And again. I used both hands

and brought the stick down with all my might. *Crack!* The
crystal shattered. The hands and face flew off. Then all the
little gears exploded apart.

"Enough!" he said, and snatched the pointer in midair.
"Now pick all that up, sit down, and *never* pull a stunt like
that a second time."

I sat there. The other kids stared at me as I felt my
power go down the drain. One kid unlatched his watch and
quietly slid it into his pocket.

I took the bus home and got off early at an open field
where there was a giant tamarind tree. I loved the tangy
flavor of tamarinds and thought they would be strong
enough to replace the burnt taste in my mouth still left over
from dinner the night before.

I searched the ground. None had fallen from the tree. I
picked up some rocks, looked around for houses, then
threw them at the pods. A few dropped down. They were
still a bit green, but I craved that sour taste. I sat with my
back against the tree and ate a bunch of them until it felt
like my face had curled inside out.

Down the street I stopped and drank from a public tap.
The water was so cold and sweet. My mouth didn't burn
and it felt good to drink water again. I drank until my belly
swelled out.

There was nothing else to do but go home. It was a long
uphill walk and I took my time. The sun was out and I was
sweating and suddenly my stomach began to roll around. I
thought maybe I would have to burp, but it wasn't that. I
could feel bits of leftover peppers and green tamarinds and
water mixing together like something fizzy and powerful.

But it didn't fizz up. I could feel it moving lower in my stomach, spinning around and around like something being flushed down a toilet. I began to walk faster. My legs felt tired. My knees were wobbly. And then I got the first hint of a loose feeling in my butt.

Oh no, I thought. The house was still two streets away. There wasn't a bathroom until I could get home. I walked faster. When I passed Shiva's house, he yelled out at me. "Hey. Do you want to go running?"

I didn't even slow down. I was concentrating on keeping my butt as tight as possible. I couldn't even shout back. I thought that if I yelled out, I'd lose control of my rear end.

"No," I squeaked. "Gotta go."

"You look a little sluggish," he yelled. "Want some prunes?"

I shook my head no.

"Well, I don't want to practice with you anymore."

I couldn't even apologize. I kept moving.

"What goes around, comes around," he said. "Think about it."

I was trying not to.

My book bag felt like it weighed a ton. I hiked up the street. My stomach rumbled. *Concentrate*, I told myself. You can do it.

I had one more street to go. I heard a car coming up behind me. It honked but I wasn't going to get out of its way. I just waved my arm for it to pass around me. As the driver swung by, he shot me a dirty look.

Don't mess with me, I thought to myself. I'll pour pee on you. But just the thought of pee made my bottom feel weaker.

I picked up speed. I balled my hands into fists of steel. I squinted. I bit my pepper-blistered lip. But the feeling in my gut grew worse, and lower. My butt began to quiver. *I can make it. I can make it. I can make it,* I thought over and over. My face was all pulled together and my rear end was so tight I walked like one of those speed walkers with my butt drawn in and my arms and legs swinging wildly for maximum forward momentum.

And then it happened. My legs got spastic, and when I tried to step around a broken bottle, I stubbed my toe and lost concentration. Whoosh! The dam broke and I felt it running through my underwear and down my shorts and down the backs of my legs. I moaned and started to run.

Hal Hunt was standing by his mailbox as I sloshed by.

"What happened to you?" he yelled. Then the smell hit him. "Ugh!" he hollered. "You smell worse than your dog."

I ran past our front gate. I couldn't go into the house. Betsy would crush me. I ran down the driveway toward the laundry room. There was a little bathroom back there. Whoosh! It hit me again. I was frantic. I opened the bathroom door. I kicked off my shoes and pulled down my pants. I slid down onto the seat and leaned forward with my head on my knees. Whoosh!

"What power?" I groaned to myself, and slapped at the flies that settled on my ears. "I don't stand a chance."

t to think about it, and I don't
t to talk about it. I don't want to touch
e pistols. I don't even want to look at
m. Most people get shot in their own
me by people they know. People like th
unt who keep bullets in their pockets a
ry and make them go off by throwing
t the ground. He is a nut. If he ha
a pistol we'd all be dead. I don't w
him. I'd rather move away. I'd rath
live on a boat in the ocean. I'd ra
be eaten by sharks than shot by
human. At least I'd die for a h
dinner. I'd rather be part of the
chain than chained to fear.

The Pistol

The house kept stinking of natural gas. Dad had checked the pilot lights on the stove and the pipe connections running from the stove to the big silver tank out back. But he could not locate a leak. It was especially strong in the afternoon. We sniffed around like bloodhounds but only found decaying bugs, mold in the corners, and bits of cruddy food under the refrigerator.

One day it was especially bad and Mom was worried that if Dad lit a cigarette the house would explode like a tanker truck, so she made him smoke out on the front porch, while she turned on all the ceiling fans. He grumbled about being booted outside, but he went, which to me meant that he thought there was something seriously wrong.

"I just want to warn you about one thing," Dad said, sitting back in his porch chair and blowing smoke rings up toward the light fixture. "A house filled with gas can be set off in a lot of ways. You don't need a match to blow up this place. The way it happens is simple. Suppose the house is filled with gas and you come home. What's the first thing you do?"

I tried hard to come up with the right answer. "When I come home," I answered shakily, "I open the door."

Dad nodded. "What's the next thing you do?"

"I turn on the lights," I replied.

"And the next?"

"I walk down to the kitchen."

"Next?"

"I turn on the ceiling fan."

Dad leaned forward and dropped his cigarette into his empty beer can and shook it around. "You'd be dead at least three different times," he said, holding up three fingers. "First, as soon as you turn on the lights, the spark from the switch would set the place off. *Kaboom!* But let's say you didn't turn on the lights. So, you walk down the hall. The little metal cleats or nails on the bottom of your shoe might give off a spark on the terrazzo floor and *kaboom!* you are dead again. But let's say you were wearing sneakers. Then when you turned on the fan, *kaboom!* Switching on any electrical appliance gives off a spark, and you are burnt toast."

"Can I use a flashlight?" I asked. I wanted to read at night without blowing myself up.

"Yeah, a flashlight is okay. Just don't drop it and break the little bulb, because the red-hot filament would set off the gas."

"What if the fillings in my teeth rubbed together in my sleep and made a spark?" I asked.

"Don't get carried away," he said, and lit another cigarette. He exhaled slowly as though he were leaking like a broken gas pipe.

Betsy was the one who solved the mystery. She walked into the kitchen a few days later and caught the new babysitter, Missy, sliding Eric into the unlit oven. She had him in a big turkey-roasting pan while the gas was turned up full-blast. It was time for his afternoon nap and she was gassing him to sleep. "Breathe deeply," Missy whispered. "For a deep, deep, deep sleep."

Betsy screamed. Missy jumped back. "I'm not doin' anything wrong," she squealed. "It's just a little gas."

Betsy snatched Eric off the oven rack. "Wait till my mother gets her hands on you," she said with authority. "She'll have you thrown in jail."

Missy turned and ran out the kitchen door and up the driveway and down the road toward the bus stop.

When Mom came home Betsy blurted out the story. "I was so angry," she said, "if I'd had a gun I'd have shot her."

Mom was horrified. "Eric may have brain damage," she cried, holding him close to her face and kissing his forehead. She pressed his little belly and smelled his mouth and nose for gas. Maybe she thought he was filled with gas and if she let him go he'd float up to the ceiling like a hot-air balloon.

"Oh, he's okay," Dad remarked, making light of her

concern as he jingled the change in his pocket. "He's one of our kids, so he's brain-damaged already."

Mom managed a strained smile. "I'll call the doctor tomorrow," she said.

"Don't you think we should call the police?" Betsy asked. "What she did was like a Nazi war crime."

"It would just be your word against hers," Dad replied. "If anything should be done, I'll do it myself. Do you know where she lives?"

We didn't answer.

"Well," Mom said, "let's not get mixed up in it. Let's just be happy that we're all fine."

But Dad did not feel fine after Stumpy Hill's house was robbed. They lived four houses down the street. A police inspector came by to ask if we had seen or heard anything peculiar the night before. I stood behind Dad when he answered the door. The inspector's uniform was gray with red piping and he wore an officer's cap with a gold police badge fastened above the visor.

"We don't know a thing," Dad replied to his question. "Didn't hear anything. Didn't see anything."

"May I have a glass of water?" the inspector asked.

"I'll get it," I said, and dashed back to the kitchen. When I returned, the inspector had taken a seat on the porch and was casually telling Dad the story.

The robber had removed the small jalousie windows over the stove and crawled in. He went to the bathroom and tied a hand towel across his face. He went into the kitchen searching for money and removed a dinner knife from a drawer. Mrs. Hill was having a sinus spell and got up to get a tissue from the bathroom. When she returned to the bedroom, the robber was going through the dresser drawers. She screamed. He turned on her and tried to hold a pillow over her face. They wrestled. He tried to slash her, but she held his wrist and pushed him back against the chifforobe. Stumpy finally woke up and joined in. Mrs. Hill was worried about him, as he had recently had a heart attack and he was panting real hard. The thief had Stumpy pinned on the floor, so Mrs. Hill yelled out, "What do you want?"

"Money," the thief replied.

She got her purse, but before she could reach in and remove her wallet, he snatched the purse and ran out the front door, vaulted over the porch wall, and vanished. After he left, Stumpy discovered that his fingers had been sliced from struggling with the knife.

The police had already found a bloody hand towel up at the corner. That's why they were asking everybody in the neighborhood if they had seen or heard anything suspicious.

"No," Dad repeated. "We didn't hear or see a thing."

The inspector finished his water and stood up. He reached into his uniform pocket and removed a business card. "If anything comes to mind," he said firmly, "give me a call. My name is Inspector Grantley."

After he left, Dad went into his office and made several telephone calls.

The next evening he came home late from work and called us into the dining room. He unwrapped a large package and removed two pistols.

"This one is for you," he said to Mom. "It's a .25 caliber revolver. And this one is for me. It's a .38."

I stared at them and stepped back. They were blue-black and big as a pair of crows. It was as though he had unwrapped something horrifying, like a human heart or severed hands. It scared me to look at them. He picked up the .38 and pointed it at the wall over our heads. I ducked down. It was the same as watching a horror movie that was too frightening. When I hid behind the seat in front of me, I had a moment of relief, but then curiosity got the best of me and I always popped up just in time to catch something brutal and bloody explode in Technicolor across the screen.

When I lifted my head again, Dad was putting the gun into Pete's hands. I ducked again.

"Cool," Pete said. He waved it around.

Dad snatched it away from him. "It's not a toy," he said. "It's something to be respected even when it's not loaded."

"I'd rather not take the law into our own hands," Betsy said and shook her head in disapproval. "Remember, those who live by the sword die by the sword."

"I, for one, will sleep a lot easier with these in the house," Dad replied and thumped himself on the chest. "And I bet Stumpy Hill wishes he had one the other night."

Mom looked doubtful. "These things lead to accidents," she said. "I just don't think they are safe."

"The only reason to be afraid of a firearm is if you don't know how to use it," Dad insisted. "So I'll give you lessons. I just want to protect the kids."

"I've never fired a pistol before, just rifles," she said, sounding like she'd give it a chance.

"There's nothing to it," Dad replied knowingly. "You just point and shoot."

After the sun went down, Mom and Dad drove out to the horse track. The racing season was over and the track was the biggest stretch of flatland where Dad could let Mom shoot at things.

When she came home, she didn't seem so concerned about having guns in the house. "Not bad," she said. "I pointed it into the night and fired a few shots. It was more like firecrackers going off."

"Did you hit anything?" I asked.

"Couldn't tell," she replied, as she unpinned her hair. "It was too dark."

The next morning I woke up when Mom screamed, "Oh my God!"

I jumped out of bed and ran into the hall, where I bumped into Pete and Betsy as we raced into the dining room. Mom was standing with her hands pressed over her mouth. She seemed frozen.

Dad was standing next to her. He rubbed her shoulders and hugged her from behind. "It means nothing," he insisted.

"*What* means nothing?" Betsy demanded.

Dad pointed at the newspaper headline. It read MAN FOUND SHOT DEAD AT RACETRACK.

"But it wasn't her," Dad said.

"What would happen if it was?" she replied.

"We'd have to sneak her out of the country," said Dad. He seemed to have already considered the possibility.

"We'd put her on a local cargo ship and send her to Brazil."

"Brazil?" I exclaimed. "Why?"

Pete was so frightened I pulled him to my side and let him hang on my arm.

"We have relatives in Rio," Dad replied, without skipping a beat.

"Really?" Betsy asked.

We had never heard about them before. I thought everyone I was related to lived in Pennsylvania.

"Yeah," Dad said. "My uncle's sister and her family went there years ago. We could put Mom up with them."

Mom looked at Dad and shook her head. "We've never even seen them, written them, talked to them, even heard of them before this moment, and you want me to go hide there like a common criminal? Have you lost your mind?"

"Do you have a better idea?" he asked.

"Yes I do," she replied directly. "I can call up the police and tell them that I may have accidentally shot that poor man."

"Wait," Betsy said, holding her hands out like a traffic cop to control the conversation. "One thing at a time. Tell me more about our relatives."

"They're rich," Dad said. "They own half of Rio. They married a bunch of Syrian lawyers and merchants and have a fortune."

Just then Eric began to cry. Betsy trotted up the hall. She returned with him pressed against her shoulder.

"Let's get back to Mom," I said. "I'm worried."

"Don't get too upset," Mom replied. "I'll just wear a

fake beard and mustache and fly back home and live in a barn with Uncle Jackson's chickens."

"Hey, let's get to the real point," Dad said. "Accidental shootings happen all the time." He snapped his fingers. At that very moment some poor guy was just walking down the street somewhere and *wham!* he was a goner.

"Once," Dad continued, "on New Year's Eve, Gooz Youski went out to his back porch and fired off a clip from his deer rifle. The next day they found some unlucky guy in the woods near Hecla shot dead with a deer slug. Same-caliber bullet. We figured it was Gooz, but nobody said anything. It was an accident. Couldn't reverse what had happened so why make it worse by sending Gooz to the slammer. Besides, we were all a little impressed with Gooz, because he had never hit a moving target before in his life." Dad smiled at his last remark. We were supposed to smile along with him but didn't.

"Well, I'm no Gooz Youski," Mom said, growing angrier and twisting out of his grip. "If I shot that poor man, I'll pay the price. I never should have let those guns into this house in the first place. I knew they would lead to trouble."

"Hey, it's not the gun's fault," Dad quickly replied.

"You're right," Mom snapped back. "It's my fault, pure and simple." She picked up her coffee cup and marched down the hall.

Dad raised his voice so she could still hear him. "Well, it would just be a manslaughter charge at best," he said. "You couldn't get much time for an accident. Maybe a year or two."

Mom stomped back up the hall and pointed her finger across the table at Dad. I was glad she didn't have her gun just then. She was furious. "Mister," she said sternly, "someone shot and killed an innocent man and it might have been me. These children," she said, and pointed at us, "may lose their mother because she listened to you. Now don't make light of this. It's serious."

Dad gazed up at the ceiling and waved his hand in front of his face like he was shooing a fly. "No big deal," he maintained. "You're making a mountain out of a molehill. You'll see."

Mom went into the bedroom. When she came out, we were still standing around the table like wax figures. "I just called Inspector Grantley," she announced. "He said he would be right over."

"I wish you wouldn't get mixed up in this," Dad pleaded. "You didn't shoot that guy. He could have been shot by anyone."

"Well, let's all get dressed," Mom said. "We don't want to look like a bunch of criminals when the police arrive."

We were waiting on the front porch when Dad turned to Mom and asked, "Where is the pistol? The cops will need to examine it."

"I threw it down the well in the back yard," she replied and turned away from him as she snapped a dead flower off a hibiscus plant.

"That only makes you look more guilty," he said and folded his hands over his head.

"I don't know if I'm guilty," she replied. "I'm scared. I just threw it down the well because I didn't want to see it anymore. And while we're on the subject, where is your pistol?"

"In my sock drawer."

"That's not much of a hiding place," she said.

"Hey," he replied. "I'm not the one who has something to hide."

Just then Inspector Grantley and his driver pulled up in front of the house. The inspector opened his door and when he stood up he stared across the roof of the car. We were all gathered on the porch, staring directly back at him. If we were in a movie, that would be the moment for a big bloody shoot-out between the Henry gang and the cops.

He walked through the gate and briskly climbed the stairs. Dad shook his hand and said, "Hell, she couldn't have shot that man. She can't hit the broad side of a barn from ten feet away."

Inspector Grantley did not seem convinced. "We'll see," he replied dryly.

He was more interested in Mom. "Where is the gun?" he asked.

She told him.

"I'll send some men around to fetch it," he said. Then he held his arm out as though he were going to ask her for a dance. "I'll have to take you down to headquarters," he said softly. "If you have a solicitor, you should call him."

Mom turned toward us with a brave face. "There is nothing to worry about. I want you to clean up your rooms. Do your homework, and if you go out to play, be home in time for dinner."

"Yes, Mom," we all murmured. We were teetering like three bowling pins about to fall over.

Then she reached for Dad's hand. He seemed to be momentarily stunned. "Aren't you coming?" she asked. He snapped to attention and led her down the steps.

Soon after they left, another carful of police arrived. I showed them where the well was in the back yard, and sat on the porch steps and waited. I didn't warn them about the bats. When one of them took a sledgehammer and hit the cement patch to widen the brick-sized hole, a tornado of bats rose up. The men bellowed and jumped back, with their faces crumpled in fear. It felt very good to watch them cower, because I imagined, at that moment, other police were scaring Mom.

In an instant the bats disappeared and the cops began to relax and laugh at themselves. I laughed along with them. Finally, they smashed open the hole and lowered a long pole with a wire basket on the end. After a few scoops through the muck, they pulled up the pistol and shook it out of the basket and into a plastic bag.

They turned and walked away, teasing each other, with their arms held over their heads like giant bats. I watched them and thought of the moment Dad brought the gun into the house. "Nothing but trouble," I said to myself.

At the end of the driveway stood Hal Hunt. He was snooping around because he had seen the police car.

"What are you spying on?" I hollered and threw a rock at him. He ducked and ran back to his yard. "Mind your own business!" I yelled.

When Mom returned in the afternoon, she showed us the black ink on her fingertips.

"Did you kill him, Mom?" Pete asked.

"I wish I knew, honey," she said, sighing. "But I don't."

"What'd they make you do?" I asked.

"Really, I just told my story to different inspectors and sat around drinking coffee until they took my fingerprints and sent me home."

"Well, when will they tell you for sure?" I pressed.

"I don't know that either," she replied. She looked more tired than worried. "I'm going to take a nap," she said. "It's been a heck of a day."

I thought if Mom went to prison I would make her a diary with a special lock and key. But it would be a trick key and she could use it to open her cell and escape. I'd meet her outside the prison and we could take a cab to the docks, untie a sailboat, and take off south for Brazil. We'd just sail right up onto the beach at Rio, call our relatives from a phone booth, and live with them. When things cooled down, we would send for the rest.

Just then Betsy opened my door. "Look," she said. "I've been thinking. If you were any man at all, you would tell the police you shot the pistol. They can't throw a kid in jail. They'll just slap you on the wrist and let you go. But they might put Mom in jail, and then what would happen to us?"

"You'd have to be the mother," I replied.

"Just think about *that*!" she said. "But seriously, what about taking the blame?"

"I can't," I said. "They'd know."

She looked me up and down. "You'd rather let your own mother go to prison than save her."

"That's not true," I replied. "I'm working on my own plan."

"What's that?"

"I can't tell you," I said. "I haven't figured out the details." I wasn't sure how big a prison key was in comparison with a diary key.

"Coward," she snapped and closed the door.

I did feel like a coward. Suddenly the diary idea seemed childish. I had to think of something else. Something that would work.

The following day Dad was still at a job when the squad car pulled up.

"Mom," I yelled and ran to the front porch.

Betsy followed. "I guess Mom did it," she said to me. "They're coming to take her away. Now's your chance to save her, unless you are as spineless as I think you are. Hurry. Throw yourself at his feet and beg for mercy."

"You do it," I shot back. "They know it was a woman who pulled the trigger."

She pinched the skin just above my hips. "Idiot," she cracked. "I'm the only girl in the family. If you got sent to prison, there would still be two boys left over."

"You're full of it," I replied and slapped her hand away.

"And another thing," she said quickly as Inspector Grantley opened his car door. "If I got sent away, this family would collapse."

Mom arrived and stood between us with her arms around our shoulders. From behind, Pete squeezed his head between our waists.

Then Inspector Grantley gave a wave of his hand and tipped his hat as he got out of the squad car, just so Mom could see his friendliness meant good news. I liked him just for that alone.

Mom exhaled and her arm felt heavy across my shoulder. I looked up at her face and caught her rubbing her eyes against the shoulder of her shirtdress.

The inspector climbed the stairs and extended his hand. "You are no longer a suspect," he said politely.

"Thank you," she said and removed her arm from my shoulder to extend her hand to his.

With his other hand he held out a small brown bag. "I'm returning your pistol. Please, don't fire it in public places," he reprimanded.

"Don't worry," she assured him. "It will never be fired again as far as I'm concerned."

Betsy stepped forward. "Well, who shot the man?" she asked.

"It was a family quarrel," he replied softly.

When the inspector left, Betsy tried to talk Mom into suing the police. Mom said she would do no such thing and sent her and Pete up to the corner store to buy formula for Eric.

As soon as they were gone she called me into her bedroom. She opened Dad's sock drawer, pulled out the .38, and lowered it into the brown bag.

"We have to throw these away," she said secretively. "Some place where your Dad can't find them."

"Okay," I replied. "But you'll have to drive."

"Honey," she said and gently touched my face, "me driving is more dangerous than me shooting a gun. Besides, you have to do it alone. Betsy and Pete will be back any minute and I have to stay with the baby. I'll call a cab."

I didn't want to do it alone, but I didn't want to be spineless either. It was my chance to save all of us from having guns in the house. "Where should I hide them?" I asked.

She opened her wallet and gave me twenty dollars. "You pick a spot," she replied. "But don't tell me where. It will have to be your secret."

I took the cab out to Needham's Point and walked out to the end of the jetty. I felt like someone was looking over my shoulder, especially with the tall lighthouse just behind me. I turned around and didn't see anyone. I could feel how angry Dad would be if he knew what I was up to. Even though he didn't know where I was or what I was doing, I knew he would soon want to know the answer to both those questions. He got upset when he found a tool out of place. He'd definitely be on a rampage when he found his gun missing.

It was dusk and the sky was more purple than orange. The waves foamed up over the ring of coral reefs just off the point. I set the bag down, reached in, and removed the .25. I stood up and winged it out there as if it were a flat rock. It hit the blue water and sank without a splash. I grabbed the .38. It was heavier. I reared back and threw it overhand. It splashed like a fish jumping. I bent down and picked up a rock and threw that, too, then another and another, as though I had been throwing rocks all along. Then I turned and quickly walked past the lighthouse, then up the road to Bay Street, where I flagged down a cab. I sat quietly in the backseat and thought, If anyone asks, I'll tell them I was throwing away my diaries so no one would read my secrets. I asked the driver to drop me off on the corner, so I could walk home as though I had been out playing.

I entered through the back door. Mom saw me before I could get to my room. "He'll be home soon," she said and kissed me on the head. "He'll be mad, but he'll get over it. Don't worry, I'll take care of you."

I nodded. I was scared speechless. Would she take care of me before or after he got to me?

Just then Dad's tires skidded to a stop as he pulled into the driveway. The door slammed behind him.

"See," he called happily after bounding up the stairs. "I told you you couldn't hit the broad side of a barn."

"Don't make a joke of this," Mom replied. "I'm still upset."

Dad picked her up by the waist and swung her around. "Let's go celebrate," he said. "We'll drive out to the Sandy Lane for lobsters."

"Oh, that would be lovely," Mom replied. She gave him a long kiss. "I've had a rough day."

"Then let's get a move on," he cried, and headed for the bedroom.

This is it, I thought. When he gets dressed he's going to go into his sock drawer. I walked down to my bedroom to wait.

I sat on my bed and timed it. He undressed. Showered. Dried off. Shaved. Opened the underwear drawer. Closed it. Opened the sock drawer.

"Where is it?" came the shout through the wall.

"I got rid of it," she said defiantly, standing up to him.

"Did you throw it in the well?"

"You told me I was stupid for doing that the first time," she said. "You'll never find it this time. Never in a million years."

He finished dressing and in a few minutes he was in my room, standing with his hand on his hip. He put his other foot up on the edge of my desk chair and tapped his fingers on the top of his knee. Betsy was right. It was my job to save Mom. But who was going to save me? If there was one less boy in the house, they would still have a family.

"You know where they are," he said. I jerked away from his eyes, but in a glance he knew that I knew something about the guns.

"Yes," I replied.

He waited for me to tell him. But I didn't.

"Your mother will tell me anyway," he said.

"She doesn't know where they are," I replied. Then added, "We're all afraid of them."

"That's nonsense. Now, you know," he said tartly, "I'll never be able to trust you again if you don't tell me."

I didn't say anything.

"I'd like to trust you," he repeated. "But you're making it hard for me." He shrugged and suddenly looked disinterested.

I thought he was going to be angry, but it was more like he was willing to give up on me, as if it didn't even matter whether he trusted me or not, when trusting a person is one of the things that matters most in life.

I stood there thinking, He's taking her to dinner and I'm taking the blame. That's not the same as saving Mom. It's more like letting her off the hook while she's feeding me to the wolves.

"I guess you are more like your mother," he said.

"I hope not," I replied.

Mom opened the door and stuck her head in. "I'm all ready," she announced.

"One minute," he replied. She closed the door. He just shook his head and slowly stepped back a few paces. Then he crouched down and held his hand on his hip like a cartoon gunslinger. I recognized the pose. We used to play "Showdown" when I was a little kid, when shooting each other full of lead was just a game.

"Get ready to defend yourself," he drawled out in a cowboy voice.

I backed away from him with my eyes on his eyes, my hand hovering over my hip. My fingers twitched.

"Draw!" he shouted as his hand came up. He pointed his finger at me and fired as I dove for cover and tumbled across the bed. I tried to draw my six-shooter but he fired again. He missed as I rolled off the bed and into the thin space between the mattress and the wall.

"I missed you this time," he growled in a varmint voice and blew smoke from his fingertip. "But I'll be gunnin' for you."

I was going to pop back up and ambush him, but he turned off the overhead light and slipped out the door. The game was over.

In a moment Mom opened the door again. "Jack," she called, in her concerned voice, "are you in here?"

I didn't answer. I stayed crouched behind the bed. I did my part, I thought. You do yours.

"Let's go," Dad hollered from the living room. "I'm hungry."

"I promise there won't be any more guns," she whispered and closed the door. I didn't move until I heard the car start. Then I crawled back on the bed. I stood and jumped up and down on the mattress. The springs creaked as I got higher and higher. I reached out in the darkness and touched the ceiling with the palms of my hands.

"I'm thirteen years old now," I said. "I bet I live to be a hundred. That's eighty-seven more years of dodging bullets."

favorite name was "Calico Jack". I'd hate to be the last guy to bury the Treasure. Usually the guy who dug the hole was shot or stabbed so he buried with the Treasure by the captain. So when M Branch finds the Treasure I'd be intere see if there is a dead pirate sprawled a

the chest. I would like to get some treasure but an old sword or some pirate bones would be

Thurston Branch

Dad's office was dark and cool and smelled like his bay-rum aftershave. He had already left the house. I slipped in and closed the door behind me. I carefully sat down in his swivel chair to keep it from squeaking. I wasn't supposed to be in there. The newspaper was spread out across his desk. I was searching for the movie section.

The front page still carried news of the drought and heat wave. It had been ninety-three degrees yesterday, and it was ninety-three days since it last rained. Everyone was worried about having enough drinking water. Most houses were built on top of a hollow cement cistern the size of a swimming pool. When it rained, the water ran off the roof, down the gutter, and into the cistern. It was good clean water, and most people used the rainwater for drinking and used well water for cleaning and watering their lawns.

"Water, water everywhere," I sang. "But not enough to drink."

I turned the page. An article was titled BOY STILL MISS-ING. A boy who lived over by Crane Bay had left his house a week ago and had not been seen since. Not a trace of him had been found. His parents were begging everyone to help. This was the third newspaper story on him. It gave me the creeps.

I didn't know how anyone could get lost on the island. It was so small, only twenty-one miles long and fourteen miles across at the widest point. It was like a freckle on the globe. Even if I got lost, broke both my legs, and had to pull myself through the cane fields with my hands, I could *still* make it back home.

I removed the scissors from Dad's desk drawer and cut out the article.

"Jack," Mom yelled up the hallway from the dining room. She was writing letters while Eric slept. "You and Pete better get a wiggle on if you're going to the movies."

I folded the piece of paper in half and shoved it into my back pocket. Then I put the scissors where I found them, so Dad wouldn't pitch a fit. Quickly, I flipped ahead to the movie section. *Them!* and *Night of the Living Dead* were play-ing. Cool. *Night of the Living Dead* was filmed outside my hometown in Pennsylvania. Maybe I'll see some of my rel-atives lurching out of their graves to eat human flesh.

I opened the door and stuck my head out. "Okay," I hollered back. It's funny, I thought, how some families actually talk face-to-face and some families just yell from room to room. And another thing, it's like when I ask Dad to hand me something, he never puts it directly into my hand. He gets about three feet away and tosses it at me like a grenade.

Mom yelled again. "Jack! You better get going!"

"I'm movin'!" I yelled back.

Pete and I were getting ready to walk down to Bay Street and catch the bus into Bridgetown. Television in Barbados was pretty lousy and they didn't run any good scary stuff. Every Saturday, the Rockley Movie Theatre played a double feature. They were mostly old black-and-white horror movies I had watched on *Creature Double Feature* back in Fort Lauderdale. The host of that TV show was a corpse named M. T. Graves. He had one huge hairy eyebrow and fake buckteeth. Every Saturday afternoon, he'd open his squeaky coffin and pop out to announce the features.

I ran up the hall and into Pete's room. "Come on," I yelled.

"I'm almost ready," he yelled back. He was standing inside his closet, searching through all his pants pockets. His pockets were supposed to be a secret hiding place, but the only secret about them was why he couldn't find anything once he hid it in them.

"The movie is going to start without us," I yelled. "And you know how I *hate* that." I jiggled the Lemon Squash bottle caps in my pants pocket. For ten bottle caps and ten cents you got to see two movies, plus there was a chance to win a door prize. We always got the bottle caps up the street at old Mr. Hill's store. He saved them for us.

"I only have eight," Pete yelled and recoiled in terror.

"Jerk," I said and squinted as I lost patience. I dashed back into my bedroom. It was like this every week. He'd

hide his bottle caps from himself, then he'd lose some, then
he'd forget his ten cents, then he'd forget money for candy,
and then I'd have to bail him out. As I opened my cigar
box, I whispered to him, "Go ask Mom for extra candy
money and meet me out front."

"Mom," he yelled as soon as he stepped into the hallway. "Can we have extra candy money?"

"No!" she yelled back. "And don't forget to brush your
teeth."

We hurried down the street but stopped when we saw a
crowd of people gathered on the Naimes' front yard.

"Maybe someone died," I said to Pete. "Let's see."

"We'll be late," Pete said.

"This is better than a movie," I replied. "This is real
life."

I grabbed his hand and squirmed through the crowd
until we came out into a clearing. I saw Johnny and asked
him what was happening.

"Mr. Branch is searching for water," he whispered as if
we were in church. He pointed at an old man who was as
thin and bent as a praying mantis. He was dressed in a
white short-sleeved shirt and brown bow tie. His hair was
cut down to the nub and the part was a sharp line that
might have been made by a bullet that just grazed his scalp.
It was hot under the sun and the sweat made shiny trails
through the dust on his outstretched arms.

"What's that thing he's holding?" I asked Johnny.

"A divining rod," he replied.

I didn't know what that was. It looked like the wishbone
from a five-hundred-pound turkey. He held the two tips of

the Y-shaped end gently between his bony fingers and closed his eyes. They fluttered as he slipped into a trance. He began to hum as he slowly inched forward. The tip of the divining rod wobbled up and down. Pete and I looked at each other, shrugged our shoulders, and followed at a distance. I didn't want to get in his way. He might trip and drive that stick right through my foot.

After a few passes back and forth across the dead lawn, the tip of the rod suddenly went straight down with so much force that Mr. Branch dropped forward on his knees. The crowd "Aahed," and a few people clapped. When he stood up, he smiled broadly and blinked sleepily at all of us who had gathered to watch him. He pulled a large white handkerchief from his back pocket and wiped his face and neck.

"There is good sweet water here," he announced, tramping the dusty ground with his foot. "Dig straight down and you will find drinking water."

Mr. Naime peeled a few crisp bills off a wad held together with a gold money clip. Mr. Branch took it, frowned, and folded it into his top pocket. "I shouldn't accept payment for this job," he said loud enough for us to hear. "God has blessed me with this power and I should only do it to help my fellow man . . . but I need the little bit of money to help out my family."

Everyone just stood limp and slack-faced after he said that. I'm not sure why. I guessed it was because he was blessed with a gift that none of us had. So if he apologized for it, who were we to argue with him?

"Allah Akbar," said Mr. Naime and spit on the ground. I suppose he was putting a little water back into the earth.

I was jealous of Mr. Branch. Finding things was the best way of getting stuff for free, and if I were him, I would run around all day finding anything I could. I'd start a business: YOU LOST IT, I'LL FIND IT! I'd take fifty percent of the value of the object found. Since school began full-time, Mr. Cucumber had been drilling us on fractions and percentages. He'd be very pleased to know that his math exercises were working for me.

Pete tugged on my arm. "Come on," he whined.

I shook him off. I wanted to get a better look at that divining rod to see what it was made out of.

Mr. Branch walked over to his tiny Morris Minor. It was a British car the size of a washing machine. He opened the door, pulled out a suitcase, set it on the ground, and clicked open the latches. The case was empty except for a bunch of soft rags, which he removed and wrapped around his divining rod before shutting it in the suitcase and sliding the suitcase back on the front seat. It looked like an ordinary tree branch. As he pulled away, we waved.

"Come on," I hollered at Pete. "We're late."

The front of the theater was decorated with a giant bottle of Lemon Squash. It was outlined in bright green neon, with little blue neon droplets of bottle sweat. Just gazing up at that bottle made me feel hotter. I was dying of thirst. The double front doors had an icy penguin on one side. On the other a sign read: COME IN. IT'S COOL INSIDE. I pushed the door open and we burst into the cold air as though with one quick step we had traveled from summer into winter.

A kid in a starched purple-and-gold uniform took our bottle caps and gave us a scrap of yellow paper with a big number hand-stamped on it. "Hang on to this," he snapped. "You might get lucky."

I stopped in front of the water fountain and drank about a gallon. The water was ice-cold and hurt my teeth, but it had been so hot outside I needed cold belly water to chill my innards. When I finished I held Pete up under his arms while he tanked up. Then we both ran up to the balcony. The wood stairs were so old it was like running up a flight of sponges.

Even though we were a little late we were still in luck. We slouched down into two seats and stared at the screen as if we were hypnotized. "What's your ticket number?" I asked Pete.

"Four," he said.

"Mine's 17."

Before each feature was a short movie of a race. They were always real old and silly like the Keystone Kops. The races were different each week. Last week it was motor-boats. This week it was cross-country horse racing. Already they were galloping across the fields and kids were shriek-ing, yelling out their horse numbers and throwing candy.

We missed the beginning, but Pete's horse was chal-lenging the front of the pack. My horse was stuck in a mud hole. The kid next to me was cheering for number 11. Secretly, I felt good when his horse took a wrong turn into an apple orchard. For a moment Pete's horse took the lead, but then his jockey got knocked off when he hit a low tree branch. My horse dragged itself out of the mud and picked up speed but then stopped at a lemonade stand. I groaned. Number 4 dove off a railroad trestle. Number 11 fell in love with a billboard of a horse. Number 2 was the winner.

A girl in the row behind me jumped up and let out a deadly scream right in my ear. "I won!" she squealed. "I won, and I've never won anything before in my life."

I elbowed Pete in the shoulder. "Time to get candy," I said. "Hand over your money." I bounced down the rickety steps, hoping to get to the refreshment counter before the line got too long.

By the time I returned, the Living Dead were already chewing on some smelly old flesh. Pete was balled up in the corner of his seat. "I just *love* a barbecue," I whispered, and passed him the popcorn.

That night I took out my diary and taped the newspaper article about the missing boy on a page. I also removed a second piece of paper from my pocket. I had gotten it at the refreshment stand when I bought my candy. It was a handbill, also about Wade Block, the missing boy. I hadn't shown it to Pete because I thought it might really scare him. There was a request for information with a police telephone number. The missing boy's mother said he was last seen on his bicycle heading for the movie theater. He was wearing a red soccer jersey with the number 8 on the front. The bike had not been found either.

I didn't know what the kid looked like but thought I would try something like Mr. Branch. I opened my diary to a clean page and took out a pencil. I shut my eyes real hard and tried to picture him. He had my brown hair and brown eyes. He was about my height. He wore that soccer jersey and shorts and tennis shoes.

With my eyes closed, I started to draw. When I finished

I looked down at the page. There he was. It was a picture of me. I'm not lost, I said to myself. I'm right here. I closed my eyes again and tried to picture the boy. But he was gone. It was as if he had turned and run out of my imagination and left me behind. I jumped up and walked around the room.

My grandfather had told me that everyone has a double on the other side of the world. Barbados, I thought, was almost on the other side from Pennsylvania, and now I wondered if that kid was my double. I closed my diary. The thought was too creepy. "You don't have a lost double," I said out loud. "You sound like Pete." But that didn't help.

I crossed the hall and knocked on Betsy's door. Whenever I had a dumb idea, she could always set me straight by making me feel so stupid I gave up on it. "Come in," she shouted.

"Can I ask you a dumb question?" I said.

"How do you know it's *only* dumb?" she replied. "It may be the stupidest thing ever uttered on this planet since the start of recorded history." She turned her book over and crossed her arms. She smiled that know-it-all smile.

"I know this sounds crazy, but do you think you have a double in the world? Someone exactly like you in . . . in every way? Looks like you? Thinks like you? Acts like you?"

To my surprise, she gave the question some thoughtful consideration instead of snorting at me. "Some people believe it," she replied. "But I don't. Mostly it's just a projection of the spiritual and emotional side of yourself."

I nodded as if I understood, but I was lost. She had been studying psychology and I figured she was studying me like Jane Goodall studied the apes.

"Tell me," she said. "Can you communicate with your double?" She peered deep into my eyes.

"I think so," I replied.

"You're schizophrenic," she said, getting slightly excited, like a mad scientist discovering a new life form. "You have a multiple-personality disorder."

"Is there a cure?"

"I . . . would . . . say," she pronounced, stretching out her words, "that, on average, people spend about ten years in a mental hospital and then they give out and commit suicide."

I blinked. "Thanks," I said weakly, and returned to my room. For once, Betsy didn't knock the idea clean out of my head. Instead, she made it worse. Now I felt like a nut case.

And I was. That night I had the scariest nightmare of my life. It was so hot I had moved to the concrete floor, which was cool with all that water beneath it in the cistern. I stretched out like a dog, belly-down, arms and legs spread apart. It felt so good. I put my head on my pillow and fell asleep. The next thing I knew I was paralyzed with fear. I heard noises in the yard outside my French doors. I tried to get up, but I couldn't move. The doors opened and a boy stepped into my bedroom. I still couldn't move; not a finger, not a toe. I couldn't blink. I felt like a frozen side of beef just lying there, waiting for a big meat hook to be driven into my shoulder. He walked forward with his arms stretched toward me like one of the Living Dead. I tried to scream but nothing came out. My jaw was frozen. I tried to move my arm but couldn't. He came closer and stood above me. I couldn't make out his face. It looked like a smeared thumbprint. He reached for me and I stopped breathing. I felt myself slowly dying. I blacked out.

When I snapped awake, I was lying on the floor in the same position as when I fell asleep. I was rigid and cold but I could move again. Slowly, I pulled my knees up, then my arms. I rubbed my face. I looked at the French doors. They were locked. Nothing had changed except for me. I got up and took a hot shower.

After I dressed I went into the kitchen. I was starving.

"What were you moaning about last night?" Betsy asked. "You sounded like a ghost with a stubbed toe."

"Just a dream," I said.

She set her toast down on her plate. "Tell me about your dream," she said. "Dreams are the keys which unlock the inner mind."

I sat down and told her everything. Every detail. I wanted her to make ruthless fun of me. To tell me I was a goon, a loser, a jerk . . . anything. But she told me just what I didn't want to hear.

"A paralyzing dream doesn't mean death," she said seriously. "It means your brain is awake with anxiety while your body is still sleeping. But I can cure you," she added. "I want you to come into my room for an hour every day and tell me honestly everything that is on your mind. If you do that, I can figure out what you're afraid of and cure you before you go around the bend and end up a vegetable for the rest of your life."

"Okay," I said. "But you can't tell anyone what I say."

"Doctors aren't allowed to tell secrets," she said and crossed her heart. She pointed up at the kitchen clock. "Meet me at three, in my room."

I took a bite of toast and nodded.

Later, Pete and I hunted for mangoes in the trees up behind Mr. Hill's store. Along the way, I told him about my dream.

"I had one, too," he said. "I told Mom and she said it was from watching too many horror movies."

"That's it?" I asked.

He shrugged. "Makes sense to me."

After I ate a pile of mangoes, I fell asleep under a shade tree and slept as soundly as BoBo II. I missed my three o'clock appointment with Betsy and woke up feeling better already. Pete was right. I was watching too many horror movies. I just needed sleep.

That evening Dad asked if we wanted to watch Mr. Branch locate Captain Kidd's pirate treasure. Pete and I kicked each other under the table. "When?" I blurted out.

"Really?" Betsy asked. "Where?"

"Sandy Lane," Dad replied. "Captain Winston Ward claims he has information that the treasure was buried there."

"Does he have a map?" I asked.

"The question should be: Does he have a brain?" Dad replied. "Imagine if you were a pirate. Would you bury your treasure on the beach? Of course not. You'd carry it inland and bury it where the shoreline wouldn't be shifted by strong tides and storms. Then you'd kill all the men who dug the holes, so they could never tell anyone. And, finally, you'd *never* make a map that someone could get their hands on. You'd keep it all in your head."

That made sense. He must have given this a lot of thought. "Then why is Mr. Branch doing it?" I asked.

"Money," Dad said. "Captain Ward said he'd give him half the treasure if he finds it."

"Wow," I said. Mr. Branch and I thought alike.

When we arrived at Sandy Lane the beach was laid out like a chessboard. Captain Ward had strung twine around pegs in the sand to mark out boxes three feet square. He had a map inside a folder that he kept checking. He wouldn't let anyone else see it. Mr. Branch sat in a lawn chair with his suitcase by his feet. He stared straight out at the horizon over the ocean and didn't pay attention to what was going on around him. He held a small Bible in his large hand and twirled it like a coin between his fingers.

After Captain Ward finished laying out his grid, he walked up to Mr. Branch and touched his shoulder. "We're ready for you," he said.

Mr. Branch slipped the Bible into his pocket, leaned forward, and opened his suitcase. He separated the divining rod from the rags and stood. He walked over to the left-hand corner of the grid, held out the rod with his fingertips, and stepped forward. I could hear the sand crunch beneath his leather shoes. No one made a sound. The waves crashed on the shore. The birds squawked. The sea-grape trees rustled their leaves, which were as round and wide as human faces. Mr. Branch marched on.

He reached the end of the first row, turned, and started down another. The divining rod didn't dip an inch. When

he reached the end of the third row, he lowered the tip of
the rod and stuck it into the sand. The crowd came to life
with little "Aahs" and "Oohs," but just for a moment. Mr.
Branch was only resting. He pulled out his big white handkerchief and wiped his face. Afterward, he picked up the
rod and marched onward.

"He can't find it," I said to Pete. "He can't *feel* it."

"Yes, he can," he replied.

"Wanna bet?"

"Whatever's in my pockets against what's in yours,"
Pete said.

"You're on." Mine were empty.

Just then Mr. Branch tripped over a twine marker and
pitched forward. I heard the rod snap as he hit the ground.
So did everyone else.

"Well, the show's over," said Mr. Steamer. He was a
rich drunk with a nose the size of a red potato. Dad had
built a bar for him in his garage.

Mr. Branch hopped up and brushed the sand off his
pants. He inspected the broken rod, then quickly split it in
half across his knee. He whipped the pieces end over end
into the ocean. A yellow dog chased after them.

"Maybe the dog'll find the treasure," Mr. Steamer
cracked.

"You!" Mr. Branch said, pointing at me. "Fetch my suitcase."

I was the closest one to it and had been thinking about
taking a peek in it when his back was turned. I picked the
case up by the handle and walked across the sand. It was
light. I carefully stepped over the strings and held it out for

him. He set it on the sand, flipped it open, and removed a second rod.

"Wow," I said.

When he looked up, our eyes locked. "It's not the rod," he said. "The power is in the man. Always remember that. The rod is just the needle on the compass. It's just a tool in the hands of power. Now go."

I turned and ran, with the bulky suitcase slapping against my thigh. I was out of breath when I reached Pete. Just then the crowd went wild. I looked over my shoulder. Mr. Branch was on his knees with the rod half sunk into the sand. He raised his free hand up over his head and smiled out at us like a matador who has just plunged his sword through the neck of a charging bull. He staggered up, then tramped the ground with his shoe. "Dig here," he called out. "I feel a powerful attraction."

Before he finished walking the entire grid, he located two more digging spots.

"The treasure must be scattered," Pete said.

"That makes sense," I said. "Spread it out, put it in different holes." Pirates were smart. They didn't want old geezers like Mr. Steamer finding their stuff.

"I won the bet," Pete reminded me.

"Which pocket?" I asked.

He thought it over. "Left," he said.

I turned my empty left pocket inside out. "Take it all," I said, and laughed.

"No fair," he whined. He grabbed the pocket and pulled.

"Let go," I yelled and swatted at him.

He held on to it like a mad dog with a bone. Suddenly there was a big ripping sound and he fell backward on his butt, holding the little piece of pocket cloth in his hands.

"Don't let Mom see that," I said. I reached over and grabbed my pocket out of his hand.

Captain Ward marched across the beach, waving his arms for attention. "Everyone, clear out!" he shouted. "We're gonna bring in lights and heavy equipment and dig through the night. We'll need some privacy when we find it." Then he smiled. "There might still be some pirates among us."

"I'm hot," Mom said. "Let's get a cool drink."

"I'm for that," Dad chipped in.

We walked the short distance to the Sandy Lane Beach Hotel. A steel band was setting up. "You kids stay out on the patio," Mom said. "We'll send out Cokes."

Betsy frowned. She hated being treated like a kid.

"The lounge is too fancy for children," Mom explained. "We won't be long." She leaned forward and kissed Betsy on the cheek. Pete ran over and got his kiss. I lined up for mine. "My God," Mom said with a sigh. "I'm only going to be twenty feet away."

As the sun went down, the steel band started up. The pan drums sounded like musical rain.

Betsy grabbed my hand. "Let's dance," she said.

"Is this some kind of trick?"

"No. I just love this dance floor."

"Me too," I said.

Dad had built the dance floor. It was made of pink-and-gray terrazzo stone that was all swirly like a giant hoopskirt spinning around. But the best part was the underground spotlights. Cemented into the surface of the terrazzo were thick glass moons and stars.

"The lights," I yelled to Pete over the music. I pointed to the switch mounted on a palm tree. He ran over and flicked it on. Suddenly moons and stars shined up into the sky like the Bat signal.

Betsy had me dancing in circles until I was dizzy and weak. "You missed your mental-health appointment with me," she said as she reeled me in.

So she did have more on her mind than just dancing. "I forgot," I said breathlessly as she spun me around.

"Forgetting is the first sign of mental illness," she said and whipped me across the floor by the wrist. She hauled me back in. "Zelda Fitzgerald was a schizoid who tried to dance her way back to mental health."

"Zelda who?" I blurted out. "Do we know her?"

"Maybe you're not a nut," she said. "Maybe you're just hopelessly stupid." She pushed me away and I tripped over a potted palm and plunged into the croton hedge. I landed on my stomach and spit up some Coke on my hand. I had to wipe it off on my little piece of ripped pocket.

What am I? I asked myself. Sick? Stupid? Or insane?

It was Monday and I was back at school, slumped down in my seat. I was exhausted. That nightmare had returned. As soon as I fell asleep, I was paralyzed. My French doors opened and a boy entered the room. I tried to move but couldn't. His face was a blur. He reached for my hands. I tried to scream. Instead, I stopped breathing. I knew it couldn't be true, but I thought I held my breath for the rest of the night.

Usually, Monday meant a lecture on how we didn't study enough, followed by a killer quiz. But this Monday was different. Mr. Cucumber started the day by handing out copies of a photograph of Wade Block. He looked exactly like the drawing I'd made. I thought of my grandfather's story about the double and I got goose bumps again. Maybe I should reschedule the appointment with Betsy, I thought. She knows a lot more than I do. I suddenly felt wide awake.

"This boy has been missing for an entire week," Mr. Cucumber said. "Do any of you know something about him?"

I raised my hand.

"Yes, Henry?"

"His bicycle is missing," I said. "He was last seen at the Rockley Movie Theatre."

"Any fool who reads the paper knows that," he replied harshly. "Do you know anything new about him? Have you seen him?"

I didn't tell him I had seen him in my mind and that I had drawn a picture of him. And that ever since he was missing I was haunted by a nightmare and was being driven insane. After his reply to the *first* answer I gave him, I figured if I told Mr. Cucumber what was really on my mind he'd turn the whole class against me.

"There is a reward for finding the boy," continued Mr. Cucumber. "If you know anything, tell your parents and call the police. And," he stressed, "if you do find him and get the reward, I expect you to donate it to the school."

Everyone groaned. Yeah, I thought. So we can hire a teacher instead of a jailer.

He placed the photograph down on his desk and picked up his math book. "Now," he boomed. "Let us review our metric tables."

During lunch I snuck around to the back of the school building. There was an empty swimming pool in the shape of Barbados. At one time it must have been beautiful. Now it was filled with dried leaves and dirt and little balled-up pieces of notebook paper. I opened my lunch bag and pulled out a small divining rod. Actually, it was a slingshot, but I had taken off the rubber straps. Still, it was the same Y shape. As Mr. Branch had said to me, "The rod is just the needle on the compass. The true power is in the man." If that was the case, I could make a rod out of a wire coat hanger. But if Mr. Branch used wood, I'd use wood. I figured he hadn't told me *everything* he knew in one sentence.

I walked down the pool steps into the shallow end, which was at the bottom of the island. I closed my eyes and concentrated. I had used a Ouija board before and thought I should ask a question, then discover the answer as I walked. "Wade Block, where are you?" I murmured. I held the rod out in front of me like Mr. Branch and took a step forward. I slowly marched up the island into the deep end. I turned and marched back. I didn't feel any downward tug. I asked the question again. "Where are you?" I rolled my eyes up into my head and paced up the middle of the island. Nothing. I turned, and as I walked back, I felt my hands jerk downward, just like getting a strike on a fishing rod. It scared me so much I yelped and jumped into the air.

When I landed, I stared down at the spot which was marked by the shadow of the rod. With my shoe I kicked away the leaves. *Castle Rock* was painted on the bottom. It was a tiny town on the edge of the Castle sugarcane plantation. Maybe he was kidnapped and hidden up there. It was pretty remote. Or maybe he was injured and no one could find him. I could save him. I'd be a hero. Then everyone would know that I had the *power* and I could start charging for finding stuff.

I went back to the classroom and studied the wall map. I took out my diary and wrote down the roads I'd have to take, then left the room before Mr. Cucumber returned and quizzed me on kilometers, sea-level elevations, latitude and longitude. He was always thinking up ways to use real life for test questions.

After school I decided to take the west coast road up the island and stop in at Sandy Lane to see if Mr. Branch had located Captain Kidd's treasure.

I rode right up to the beach and walked my bike along the sand. Mr. Branch was standing on the edge of one of the holes while mindlessly twirling that little Bible through his fingers like a magician. All the lights and digging equipment were gone. Next to the NO TRESPASSING sign was a tourist with a metal detector. Mr. Branch sneered at him.

"How'd it go?" I asked.

He turned and recognized me. "Witness it with your own eyes," he said sadly.

I looked down into the hole. The sides were lined with plywood and shored up with two-by-fours to keep the loose sand from caving in. It was about fifty feet deep and half filled with water.

"Saltwater," he said. "It's like rubbing salt in a wound. This is a puzzlement to me. This is the first time I haven't found what I'm looking for. I guess God didn't mean for me to find a treasure that was ill-gained. I guess that was it. For punishment he took my power away."

I looked down into the other two holes. There was nothing but water. "Maybe you're just really good at finding water," I said, trying to sound positive.

"Not so," he replied. "I'm a finder. I find things. Anything. Like that missing boy. I'm going to find him for the family. God will restore my power when I put it to good use."

"I read about him in the paper," I said. I pulled the picture out of my pocket and unfolded it. "We got this in school. There's a reward."

"Reward?" he asked. "How much?"

"I don't know," I said.

He lifted the paper out of my hand and stared at Wade Block. He closed his eyes and placed the palm of his hand on Wade's face. He threw his head back and concentrated on something only he could see. "What do you know about this?" he asked and stared down at me with his wide eyes bugged out like a horror-movie madman. "Tell me!" He put his hand on my shoulder. "I *feel* that you know something."

"Nothing," I replied. I backed away from him. "I don't know any more than you do."

"You're lying," he snapped.

I couldn't tell him about the drawing and the nightmare. "I have to go," I said.

"Well, I have to find him," he insisted, and poked himself so hard in the chest I thought he was going to knock himself backward into the hole. "I must prove I've got my power back. That Captain Ward called me a fraud. He can't call me that. God gave me the power to find things. If he calls me a fraud, it's like calling God a fraud." He was shouting.

I turned and picked up my bike. "Good luck," I said. I walked to the road and took off for Castle Rock. I glanced over my shoulder to make sure he wasn't following me like some fiendish stalker with a machete the length of my arm. But he wasn't that kind of a stalker. What really scared me about him was the same thing that scared me about Betsy. That both of them could just look at me and see into my own mind, spy on my thoughts and feelings, and read me like a book.

I wanted to know if I had the power to see and feel things that other people could not. Once I ordered a pair of those X-ray glasses advertised in comic books. But they were fake. I couldn't see anything past my nose. Even back then I knew I couldn't get power from a gimmick. Power was drawing that boy's face in my diary *before* I saw the photograph. I hadn't figured out what the nightmare meant yet.

I pedaled as hard as I could against the traffic. The roads were narrow, and every time a car passed by, the wind pushed me toward the open gutters. If I fell in, I'd crash and be covered with sewage. I passed rows of wooden chattel houses and hotels. I continued up past Alleynes Bay, Read's Bay, and Mullins Bay. I looked at my watch. I was making good time. If I found the kid I'd be a hero and wouldn't have to worry about when I got home. If I didn't find him, I'd have to pedal like a fiend to get back in time for dinner.

At Speightstown I turned up Highway 1 toward Castle Rock. There was less traffic, but the roads were steep and uneven. The cane was low. Without water the crop was stunted. At Portland Plantation I stopped by a store and drank from the tap. It tasted rusty. I was tired but didn't have time to rest. I hopped on my bike and kept going. After Diamond Corner I took a left toward Castle Plantation. Castle Rock was a town made out of old slave quarters. I pulled over and stopped. I reached into my backpack and took out the little divining rod and held it in my hands. "Wade Block," I murmured. "I'm here to find you. Speak to me."

I waited a moment. Nothing. "Speak to me," I said. Nothing happened. I put the rod away. Then I headed into Castle Rock. There was only one road. "Speak to me," I whispered. I waved to an old couple sitting on a porch. They waved back. Then I saw the boy. Someone had painted the image of a soccer player on the side of an aboveground water tank. But they had only painted his outline in big white brush strokes. A number 8 was painted on his chest. The soccer ball was at the tip of his foot. The face was a white smudge, as if someone had painted a face they didn't like and tried to rub it off with a rag. When I saw it, I knew it was my nightmare. I could feel my skin crawl. The hair on my head became spiky. My muscles stiffened up. Get out of here, I said to myself. Before you're so paralyzed you fall over and can't roll out of the way of a car. I stared up at that smudged face and felt my throat tighten. I jerked my head away, stood up on my pedals, and sped back through Castle Rock. I took a left on Highway 2-A and cut through the middle of the island, past acres of cane fields and row after row of royal palms. Wade Block, I thought, you're scaring me to death.

I got home in time for dinner. Dad was in a great mood. "I ran into Captain Ward," he said. "He was a mess. He was down at the Pig's Ear having bacon, eggs, and beer for breakfast. He'd been up all night. They didn't find a cent. It cost them a bundle to rent the backhoe for the night, but he was laughing about it. Said it was a great time. When the sun was rising they sat on the shore singing, Yo-ho-ho and a bottle of rum. I guess if you have the money, you can spend your life digging in the sand like a kid with a bucket." He was smiling. I knew he wished he was there with them. This was just the kind of adventure he'd go for. Me too. We both liked to find things. Maybe we would have been pirates together if given the chance. As it was, we were already living like pirates, landlocked pirates, moving from different towns and countries, searching for the easiest way to earn a quick fortune.

That night Betsy woke me up. When I opened my eyes, she had her hand clamped over my mouth.

"You're having a nightmare," she said. "Calm down."

It had returned. I thought I had prepared myself against it. I had stacked a bunch of empty tin cans by the French doors, so if they opened, they'd make a huge noise. Plus, I fell asleep with a flashlight in my hand. It was still there. I was so paralyzed with fear I couldn't turn it on.

"I need to work on you," she said. "Before it's too late."

"I'll be okay," I said.

"It's your funeral," she replied. "I really *don't* know

what's wrong with you, but you'd better get outside help."

I need to find Wade Block, I thought. I won't rest until he shows up. When she left the room, I sat up in bed with the light on. I felt a little better. Betsy didn't really know what was wrong with me. She was brainy, but didn't have that much *power*.

I was still awake when the newspaper arrived. The Wade Block story had made it onto the front page. It was announced that Mr. Branch had entered the search. He had already found the bicycle in Holetown. He was quoted as saying he expected to find the boy shortly. I turned the page to continue the story. There was that photograph of Wade Block wearing a soccer shirt with a number 8 on the front. I got goose bumps the size of bee stings. My hair felt like needles digging into my scalp. I threw the paper down and ran to my room.

After I got dressed I taped my divining rod to the top of my bicycle headlight and took off down the road. I wondered what might happen if the rod suddenly pointed down. Maybe I'd fly over the handlebars.

Nothing scary happened until I arrived at school and Mr. Cucumber gave us a pop quiz. He had devised a set of Wade Block math problems to test us on kilometers and geometry. One of the questions read: If Wade Block was riding his bicycle in a perfect circle at ten kilometers per hour and the police were driving in a perfect isosceles triangle where all points touched within the circle, at what speed would the police have to travel to intercept young Block at the third point?

I read it and put my head down on my desk. He was heartless.

"Is this how you behave in the United States?" Mr. Cucumber asked, as he patrolled for cheaters.

"No sir," I replied. "I just don't know the answer."

"Perhaps you did not study your math and geometry," he suggested. Then he turned to the class. "Can anyone help Master Henry solve this problem?"

Four hands shot up into the air.

I shook my head. Nothing is going to be solved until they find that kid, I thought. I'm thinking about life and death and he's thinking circles and triangles. We are worlds apart.

I took an F on the test.

After school, things got worse. I was pedaling down Rockley Road when Mr. Branch pulled up alongside me.

"You," he hollered out his window.

He startled me. I jerked my wheel to the right and almost slipped into the gutter.

He nodded toward the divining rod taped on my headlight. "Don't fool with God's power," he shouted. "It's dangerous."

"I just want to help out," I yelled back.

He reached out the window and pointed his long bony finger at me. "Stay out of the way," he said sternly. "You don't have the power. I've already delved into your spirit. It's not in you. You only have fear."

"You just want the reward," I shot back. "You don't care about the kid."

"That's a lie," he shouted furiously. He snatched one side of the Y on the divining rod and gunned his engine just as I hit the rear brakes. The rod split in half like a wishbone as he swerved to avoid a car, then sped away. I was left with the big piece and made a wish. "I hope one of us finds you soon," I said to Wade Block. "I can't sleep at night and now I have a maniac after me during the day."

The rest of the week I didn't do anything after school but ride around with my map of the island and cross off streets that I investigated. But I didn't get a nibble. The newspapers continued the Wade Block report and every day the reward grew larger. The police were out combing the cane fields. They were checking the beaches to see if he washed up. Dogs were called in. Wells were examined. The radio and television asked for volunteers to search every square inch of the island. Still, they couldn't find him. I couldn't. It was up to Mr. Branch and he was waiting for the reward to go sky-high. He had the power, but he was just sitting on it. I was sure of it.

On Saturday I snuck back into Dad's office. The newspaper was on his desk, where it always was. I leafed through the pages. I read the headlines of every article. There was nothing about Mr. Branch or Wade Block. I knew they hadn't found Wade yet, because he was still finding me. I had hardly slept a wink. Toward the back of the papers were the movie listings. *Mothra* and *Invasion of the Body Snatchers* were playing.

It was still too early to wake Pete. I went out to the back yard and with a stick drew a map of Barbados in the dirt. "One more time," I said with the half a divining rod in my hands. "Wade, where are you?" I stepped into the map. The rod went straight down. "He's in Bridgetown," I said. "Castle Rock was just a runaround."

I hopped on my bike and sped down our street. I took a

right at the bus stop and followed that route to Trafalgar Square. I locked my bike to the steel fence around the statue of Lord Nelson. Then I ran the rest of the way.

When I arrived at the theater, the neon lights were off. An ambulance was parked out front. On the corner I could see Mr. Branch's Morris Minor half parked on the sidewalk. A few people stood around the ambulance. They didn't look official, so I pushed open the front door with the chilled Penguin and went in. It was *not* cool inside. It was hot and muggy and greasy-smelling and something else, something nasty. The lobby was empty. I went over to the drinking fountain.

Just then the inner door to the seats was pushed open from behind. Mr. Branch stepped forward. "Don't drink from that water," he said sternly. He held out his hand as if he could control me from the other side of the room. But he didn't have that kind of power and I was thirsty.

I leaned over the water cooler.

"Don't!" he shouted. "It's tainted."

I stopped. Behind him I heard the stretcher wheels wobbling up the aisle. Farther back, someone was crying. Mr. Branch held the door open for the ambulance crew. When they came into sight I knew I would never speak with Wade Block or ever see him again in a dream. It was over. Mr. Branch lowered his head and made the sign of the cross. He could see everything in his mind, but I could not. I had to look. Wade's body was zipped up in a thick plastic bag like a fancy suit. Water trickled from a hole in the side. The smell was hideous. I pulled the rim of my T-shirt up over my nose.

His parents walked by. Both of them had their hands

pressed over their red faces. Tears ran down their cheeks and chins and left dark drops of water on their shirts.

Mr. Branch drifted across the lobby and stood next to me. "I found him in the cistern," he said quietly. "He was wearing a bathing suit. During the movie he must have slipped through a hole in the floor to take a swim. A lot of boys do, but this one got lost."

"How do you know?" I asked.

"I just do," he replied. "*I* have the power."

I didn't. I didn't know what I had. I could see things, but maybe that wasn't special. When I closed my eyes, I saw Wade in the darkness calling out for help. But with the movie and the screaming kids he couldn't be heard. But what I saw didn't need a special power. Anybody could see that, if they closed their eyes and thought about it. Anyone who wanted to help. And I did. If I was down in that hole I'd want some boy looking for me. I'd tried, but I was too late.

...s the people in the house were okay. ...en we were standing on the road looking ...n into the gulley, I kept wondering. Did ...have the engine running? Or was he ...sting down the hill? Was he trying t... ...l better about something that was bot... ...g him? Or was he just driving like ...aniac? Maybe someone was chasing h... ...someone who wanted their money. Beca... ...re must have been going pretty fast ...left the road and hurled through t... ...and landed roof down on the other si... ...in a gulley and right next to a li... ...wooden house. But he didn't get ...The car looked like a beer can so... ...had stepped on and he just cr... ...out. He's like some kind of rubber

I was in the back yard trying to build muscles. I looked like a skinny boy, but before long I planned to bulk up like a man. First, I did fifty sit-ups, then ten chin-ups and twenty push-ups. Dad had an old cannonball that he had uncovered at the beach while digging a luau pit. I picked it up and held it against my chest and groaned out loud as I did deep knee bends until my thighs burned. I completed ten more chin-ups and had just dropped down from the bar when Cush pulled up the driveway. He was a friend of Dad's. Mom called him a "shady character."

"Who can tell how he makes a living?" she had once remarked. "He's on the golf course all day, and out cattin' around all night."

I had never seen Cush work, but on my birthday last month he had given me a twenty-dollar bill. It was none of my business how he got his money as long as some made it into my hot hands. Now he was driving a new green-and-white Triumph two-seater sports coupe. The engine purred, and after what Mom had said, I began to think of him as a cat. A shaved cat who wore a lot of English Leather cologne.

"Hey, buddy," he hollered as he hopped out of the Triumph. He ran at me as though he were in a rush. He was wearing a bright orange suit with a yellow shirt, and a sky-blue scarf knotted around his neck. He had on a pair of white leather loafers and a matching white belt. "Is your dad home?"

"No," I replied, and shielded my eyes. "He's in Saint Lucia trying to drum up business." Dad had talked a cruise line into letting him travel between the islands while he gave cocktail talks on buying property and homes in Barbados. The hotel-building business had dropped off and he was working a "new luxury-home market," as he put it.

"That's right," Cush said, groaning. "I forgot he took off. I sure need his help." He cracked his knuckles and did a little drumbeat on the side of his leg. He was so bright and jumpy he made me nervous.

"Well, can I do something?"

That cheered him up. "Listen," he whispered. "You're as smart as your old man. You like a good deal when you hear it—well, here's the story."

His enthusiasm hooked me even before I heard a detail. "Do you still have that twenty dollars I gave you?"

"Yeah," I replied.

"Well, now you're in luck!" He jabbed me in the belly. "Hey," he said, stepping back in mock fear. "That is some *hard* belly."

Even before he asked me I rolled up my sleeve and showed him my biceps.

"You put Popeye to shame," he cracked. "But here's the difference. Smart guys like us crave greenbacks, not spinach."

I agreed with that. "You bet," I said. "I like greenbacks." If I wanted to be a real man, I needed real money.

"Now, you loan me that twenty and I'll give you forty tomorrow."

That *was* a good deal. A one hundred percent return in one day, I figured. Mr. Cucumber would be proud of my math skills.

"Well? I'm waiting for an answer. You'll never find a better deal worldwide. I can promise you that. And to earn it," he said, squeezing my arm, "you don't have to move a muscle."

"Okay," I said eagerly. "I'll go get it."

He looked up over his shoulder at the kitchen window. "Hurry," he whispered. "I don't want your mom messing up this golden opportunity."

"Don't worry," I replied. "She's at her new job."

I ran directly to my room and pulled the twenty out of my diary. When I returned, he was already sitting in his Triumph. He gave the engine a little gas. The fenders twitched just like his head and shoulders.

"Thanks, buddy," he said, and plucked the twenty out of my hand and folded it into his shirt pocket. Then he reversed in a fast, straight line, curled out onto the road, and slipped into first gear.

I walked up to the front porch singing "Forty bucks, forty bucks . . . I love the sound of forty bucks."

Betsy was sitting there with a book on her lap. The pages fluttered and buzzed with the wind. "What did he want?" she asked.

"He was looking for Dad."

"Did he ask you for money?"

"No."

"Your nose is growing," she said sarcastically. "Don't lie to me. He's a sleazeball. He owes money to everyone and now he's taking money from you."

He's got money, I thought. *My* money. But I'll double it in my sleep. I didn't want to tell Betsy about our deal, but I wanted to bug her, so I said, "You just have a crush on him, but he already has a girlfriend. She's a singer at the Colony Club."

Betsy glared at me. "You know nothing," she snapped. "She said good riddance to him weeks ago."

"Well, since you know everything already," I trilled, "there is no reason to ask me questions." I turned and smartly strolled down the hallway.

"Sucker! Don't say I didn't warn you," she hollered.

Back in my bedroom, I flipped through the sections I had marked out in my diary. DAD HORROR STORIES, LOTTERY TICKETS, DREAMS, POEMS, PERSONAL, JUNK, SONGS, PETE, until I arrived at MONEY. I wrote down CUSH— $20.00. Then I wrote down beneath it, REPAID—$40.00. As soon as I wrote the last zero a voice in my head cautioned: Don't count your chickens before they hatch. It sounded like Dad's voice.

After school, I was standing behind the garage with Mom's cloth tape measure draped over my straining biceps. I read the results. My muscle hadn't grown one bit. Just then I heard a car crunching the gravel in the driveway. I peeked around the corner. It was Cush. He had cut the engine off and was coasting in with my forty bucks.

"I don't have it yet," he said when I leaned against his open window. "The guy is out of town. But I have a better deal for you. Let's say you have the forty bucks already. Let me have it for another night and I'll double your money. So, when I pay you back, I'll give you . . ."

"Eighty," I answered. That was a lot of money. "Okay."

"Double or nothing it is," he said smoothly.

"What do you mean by *nothing*," I asked.

"Hey, pal, your money is riding on a bet. You don't think you can double your money by playing tiddledywinks? You have to take some risks if you want to make money with the big boys. I bet your twenty bucks at a cockfight and we won. And when we win, *you* win."

"But . . . I thought you had borrowed my money. Doesn't that mean you take the risk?"

He drummed his fingers on the steering wheel. "Hey, partner, don't get cold feet. You and I are going to make a lot of money off that twenty-dollar bill. Now just be patient." He swung his door open and stepped out. "Here," he said, pointing at me. "Let me give you some muscle-man lessons. It'll help keep you from worrying to death over a measly twenty bucks."

"Eighty," I said.

"Whatever," he replied.

I didn't know what else to say about my money and I figured he must know something about muscles. Anyone who doesn't pay his debts on time must be tough.

"First," he instructed, "take a roll of kitchen plastic wrap and wrap it around your whole body like a bag of leftovers. 'Course, don't cover your face. Then you have to run a mile. This will cause you to sweat like a fountain and will melt down all your fat. Then you have to eat a lot of bananas and drink fruit juice. *Only* after this conditioning," he stressed, "are you ready to lift weights." Suddenly he shot his arm forward and looked at his watch. "But right now I have to get movin'," he said quickly and turned toward the Triumph. "It's time to collect some of our money."

I didn't want to slow him down. "Okay," I said.

"By the way," he asked, and stepped back toward me. "Do you have any more money?"

"I have another twenty."

He grinned. "Well, buddy. Go get it! That twenty is just sitting around doing nothing. Let me put it to work and I'll double that for you, too."

I ran into the house counting to myself. Twenty to forty, to eighty, to one hundred and sixty, to three hundred and twenty, to six hundred and forty. I was going to have a big stack of money. By the time Dad returned I'd be loaded. I could quit school and go into business with him.

Betsy was waiting for me outside my door. "Could you do me a favor?" she asked.

"Like what?"

"Give Cush this note."

I knew she had a crush on him. "What'll you give me?" I asked coyly.

"Some good advice."

"Like what?"

"You'll have to give it to him first."

Just then I heard Cush start up the Triumph. "Okay," I said. "Okay." I snatched it from her hand and went into my room. I got the twenty out of my diary and ran back to Cush.

"Thanks, pal," he said, and shoved the bill up above the sun visor. "See you soon." He started to back away.

"When?" I asked.

He shrugged.

"Wait, I've got something else for you," I said and reached into my pocket.

He hit the brakes. "More cash?"

"Just a note," I said, and handed it to him.

"Later, buddy," he said and pulled away.

"Well?" Betsy asked, when I returned to the house. "Did he read it?"

"He wouldn't open a love letter in front of me," I said in a sappy voice.

"It wasn't a love letter," she replied. "It was a warning to leave you alone."

"Well, I'm old enough to take care of myself," I shot back. I was so angry. She'd made me look like a baby.

"But you aren't old enough to know when you are being taken for a ride," she said, sounding so old, so wise, so snotty.

I stomped into my room, opened my diary, and counted my imaginary money.

The next day I was wrapped in clear plastic and running circles in the back yard when Cush glided up the driveway.

"I know you are the nervous type when it comes to

money," he said, flipping open the Triumph door and swinging his legs out to stretch them. "So I just wanted to come by and put your fears at ease."

I stuck out my dripping hand for a payoff.

He shook it, then wiped his palm on his pants leg. "I don't have the cash," he said. "I had to reinvest it."

I looked down at my feet. The sweat was leaking out of my plastic and filling up my sneakers. "You aren't taking advantage of me?" I asked.

"Don't you go believing your sister," he said, nodding toward the house. He had read her note. "If I was going to gyp you, I'd just not show up. I'd leave town. Cut out."

"Well, when do you think you can get the money?"

"Here's the deal. I bet our money at the cockfights. I got a guy there named Otis who gives me inside tips and we are just slowly setting everyone up to make a big bundle. I've been losing a little cash just to let the regulars think I'm an easy target. But then we'll suck them into one big bet and end up with a wad of cash as thick as your leg."

I peered down at my leg. It wasn't thick enough.

"Take that plastic off," he said. "You look like you're melting."

"I am," I said, puffing.

He stood up. "It's time for me to give you more muscle training. Now, what you do is this. Get two empty paint cans and a six-foot piece of steel bar. Then mix up some quick-acting concrete and fill one can, then jam the rod down into it and let it sit for a minute and get hard while you mix up the next batch of concrete. Then, when the first concrete sets up, do the other side the same way. Once you make the barbell, then I can really show you how to bulk up." He rolled up his sleeve and made a muscle. "Feel this," he instructed.

His biceps looked like a knotted rope under his skin.

"Hard as steel," he claimed. "When I finish with you, you'll be strong and rich, and, buddy, that's all you need in life."

I grinned. Strong and rich, I thought. Strong and rich. I loved the sound of those two words lined up shoulder to shoulder.

He started the engine. "Later, partner," he said, gave me a snap salute, and pulled away.

I went around to the side of the house and entered my room from the French doors. I undressed and wrapped a towel around my waist. I needed to take a shower. I smelled like old leftovers from all that sweating. When I opened the bedroom door, Betsy was standing there.

"*When I finish with you, you'll be strong and rich,*" she sang, parroting Cush.

"You spied," I yelled.

She didn't care.

"So what? You should be disgusted with yourself," she continued. "Mom said he spends his money on cockfights. That's animal abuse, and now you are part of it. You should be ashamed."

"He does not abuse animals," I said.

"Now you are lying," she shot back. "You lie because you are guilty and you know it."

"Okay," I conceded. "You're right. He's betting it at the cockfights. But it's no worse than eating chicken for dinner."

"Listen to what you are saying," she said bitterly. "What's gotten into you? You're behaving so strangely.

You've fallen behind in school. You don't have any friends, and now you're hanging around with some criminal."

"He's not a criminal," I replied.

"What he does to those animals is criminal," she shot back. "They let those cocks fight to the death for entertainment. You are making *blood money* off of innocent animals. Plus, it's illegal. Doesn't that bother you? How can you sleep at night?"

I slept just fine. Every night I fell asleep counting my money. More money than I had ever held at one time. More money than I had ever seen. I was raking in those bills as though I was raking leaves into a big heap. I rolled around in it, smelled it, and fell asleep on it. If I was losing sleep it wasn't over the cockfights, it was because Cush hadn't paid me yet.

"Just mind your own business," I said.

"People like you and Cush should be taken out and horsewhipped!" she declared, and stomped up the hall.

I was in the back yard mixing concrete in a bucket when I heard someone whistle. I looked up and it was Cush. I put down my trowel.

"Any luck?" I asked.

"Well, I still don't have your money. But I have the proposition of a lifetime. I owe you around two hundred bucks. For three hundred dollars we can buy our own fighting cock and then split the winnings. This way, we can make the big money. What do you say?"

I thought about it. "Where do we get the other hundred?"

"I'll throw in a hundred."

"Then I should get two-thirds of the profit," I pointed out.

"You drive a hard bargain," he remarked.

"I'm in this for the money," I said, saying something he might say.

"You sound just like your old man," he replied. "I like that. Right now, I've got to go take care of business. And by the way, I'll pick you up on the corner tomorrow at three and we can drive out to the cockfights and clean house."

"What's a cockfight like?" I asked.

"Ah, they just kick the stuffing out of each other. Only lasts about fifteen seconds."

"Betsy said they're pretty bloody," I said. "She said it's animal abuse."

"Has she ever seen one?" he asked. "I bet not."

I shook my head. "I don't think so."

"Well now, who are you going to believe? I've seen 'em a hundred times and I tell you they aren't so bad. Sure they get scratched up, but a real man doesn't faint from the sight of a little blood. Right, buddy?"

"Right," I replied.

"Now, don't let her butt in," he whispered. "This is for *men* only. She's just jealous because she's not in on this deal."

I nodded.

He backed out of the driveway and vanished.

The next day he was right on time. The moment it was three o'clock, he pulled up. I hopped in and we cruised down the road.

"Nice outfit," I remarked. He was dressed in a pink-and-white-striped suit. He had a white shirt with big green-and-black diamonds across the chest. On his head he had a new white cap.

He smiled. "Thanks," he said proudly. "I just bought it."

I was wearing an old pair of khaki pants and a T-shirt. I knew blood stained, so I didn't want to wear anything that would make Mom suspicious.

"So," he started up. "Have you figured out how you are going to spend your money?"

"Thought I'd save it," I replied.

"Oh, you are one of *those* guys," he remarked with a sneer. "Too cheap to puke."

"What's wrong with saving money?" I asked.

"Money is to be spent," he replied. "It was made for using, not for hoarding. If you are already a penny-pinching cheapskate at such a young age, you'll be an old tightwad when you grow up."

"Well, I thought I would save up for a motor scooter."

"Skip the scooter," he advised. "Buy a Harley. That's a man's machine. Those scooters are like riding a hair dryer on wheels."

"What are you going to do with your money?" I asked, wanting to change the subject.

"Me? I'm going to throw a huge party and invite everyone I owe money to. And when they are all drunk, I'm gonna stand on the dining-room table and tell some jokes, and when they're in a great mood, I'm gonna tell them that the party is their payment and that having a good time among friends is better than having all the money in the world."

"Do you think they'll go for that?"

"Sure," he replied. "Who wouldn't?"

"Well, I wouldn't," I said. "I'd rather have the money than a party."

Cush reached across me and popped open the glove box. He removed a thin silver flask. "You want a drink?" he asked as he unscrewed the top.

"No, thanks," I replied. "I don't drink and drive."

"Knucklehead," he said. "You aren't driving."

"Knucklehead," I shot back. "I'm only thirteen."

He threw his head back and laughed.

I did the same. It felt good to laugh at something stupid, and feel free to say anything that came to mind. I didn't have to consider the *right* answer or the *best* or *safest* answer. Whenever I said something at home I had to defend it, explain it, and generally feel as though my whole life was a pop quiz. Whatever I said to Cush seemed just fine. Maybe this is what it's like to be a man, I thought. I can finally say and do anything I want. It was worth risking the forty bucks just to feel this free.

Cush took a sip from his flask and almost spit it out when I said, "I want a tattoo."

"You're a kid!" he shouted, pushing my words back at me.

"So?"

"So, you'll regret it," he said. "Look, when you have a crazy idea like getting a tattoo, you have to do something equally crazy to drive it out of your mind."

"Like what?"

He swerved so hard to the left that I lurched sideways and bounced my forehead off the steering wheel. He gunned the engine, downshifted, and we tore up the side of Chalky Mountain, picking up speed all the way.

"Hang on," he shouted as we reached the crest and dove over.

The road dropped away beneath us. All four wheels of the Triumph left the ground as we kept going up into the air. Then we nosed forward and came down with a hard jolt. My head hit the ceiling. Cush shifted into neutral and turned the engine off. The Triumph picked up speed as we tilted downhill. When we reached the flat part of the road, we coasted silently past rows of royal palms and harvested cane fields, string beans, and banana trees until ever so slowly the Triumph lost its velocity, and like a toy pushed across the floor, we finally rolled to a stop.

"Take a deep breath and listen to the birds," Cush instructed.

I did. The crows were calling each other. The finches were twittering. The egrets were chuckling as they pecked insects off the field plants.

After a moment he asked, "Do you still want a tattoo?"

"No," I replied.

"I didn't think so," he said. "Every time I feel like doing something nuts I drive fast, then slowly coast to a stop, and by then that crazy feeling is gone. You know what I mean? Like now, I just feel calm, cool, and collected."

I did, but it didn't last long enough. Just when I was try-ing to feel free and easy and listen to the birds, I thought about my money. Dad always said only rich people and fools didn't worry about money. I guess I wasn't either.

And I was also worried about Cush. He could owe people money, spend wildly, and still relax. I didn't owe a cent and I was nervous about everything. I didn't think he was rich, so maybe he was a fool.

"You ready to kick some butt?" he asked.

"Ready," I replied.

"Then put your game face on," he said and passed his broad hand across his face. As he did so his expression changed from carefree to deadly serious.

"Let's clean house," he cried out, and started the engine.

In a few minutes we arrived at a sugarcane plantation. We drove down a red dirt path that was rutted from heavy trucks. On either side the green sugarcane stretched out in rows. It looked like corn.

Where the cane stopped, we pulled up to an old stone bull pen. Cars and trucks were parked every which way around the tall walls. There was a solid wooden gate that was so large there was a small human-size door built into it. Cush knocked rapidly on the door. It opened a crack, then all the way.

"Cush man!" shouted a jolly voice. "Come in."

I stepped in behind him.

"Jack," Cush said, "this is Felix. Felix, this is my partner, Jack."

We shook hands. "Hope you brought lots of money," Felix said.

"I plan to leave with more than I arrived with," I replied.

"*That* is why he is my partner," Cush said gleefully, and slapped me across the back. "Now let's go find our golden goose."

To one side of the bull pen was a circular pit surrounded by rickety bleachers. They were already half filled with men shouting bets at each other while waving thick wads of money in their hands. Other men ran around recording the bets in little black books.

On the opposite side of the pen was a gathering of owners, trainers, and cages filled with princely strutting cocks. Cush waved me along.

"This is Otis," he said, introducing me to the trainer. Then he pointed at the rooster. "And this is Cash, the king of fighting cocks. Nice name, huh?"

I nodded.

He squatted down to look at the cock. It had clipped rusty feathers, a fluffy white neck, and a bouquet of black plumes bristling up from its tail. Its head was blood red and chopped the air like a hatchet blade as it pecked the wire cage. It paced back and forth on long strong legs with wide yellow feet. It looked mad. It looked like it was *always* mad.

"Bet everything you got," Otis suggested. "It's feeling strong today." He held out his arm and showed us a row of peck marks.

"That's all I need to know," Cush replied, looking up at him. "Let's go all the way." He took a balled-up handkerchief out of his jacket pocket. He opened it and handed Otis a pair of shiny spurs. "I sharpened them myself," he said.

Otis held one up to the light. They were razor-sharp

blades mounted on a steel cuff small enough to fit around Cash's legs. "Nice job," he remarked. "I'll get him ready."

We took our seats on the bleachers and waited. There were no other kids. There were no women. There were just men and they were busy arguing and exchanging money.

"Let me do the talking," Cush said as his eyes swiveled back and forth. "These guys are cutthroat bettors." When he saw someone he knew, he stood up and carefully tiptoed through the crowd.

As soon as he was gone a man turned to me. He had one cloudy eye and was missing most of his teeth. He ran a long dirty finger across his wrinkled throat. "Cush's Cash is a punk bird," he pronounced. "You'll be roasting him for dinner."

"Thanks," I said timidly.

"You want to make a bet?"

"No," I replied. "Cush handles all my money."

He threw his head back and laughed like a maniac. I turned away.

When Cush sat down he leaned forward and whispered into my ear. "This is better than I ever could have imagined," he said. "We're going to need an armored car to get all the loot home."

His confidence made me feel a little better.

Suddenly the crowd stood up. The first match was about to begin. Two trainers entered the ring and held the cocks while an assistant crimped the long, razor-sharp spurs onto their legs. Then they tied their feet together with a leather strap to keep them from kicking. The referee gave a signal and the trainers held the two opposing cocks beak to

beak and let them peck at each other until they were furious. When they seemed almost insane with anger, the referee gave a hand signal. The trainers quickly removed the
leather straps, and, spurs first, they lobbed the cocks into
the middle of the ring.

The fight lasted less than a minute. They kicked at each
other, cackled, and fluttered around. Feathers darted
through the air. The razor-sharp spurs flashed. Blood
spurted out of the wounds. The crowd thundered. Then it
was all over. The owner of the brown cock named Lady
Rose jumped up and called it quits. In order to stop the
fight the trainer threw a fishnet over both cocks. The assis-
tants pounced on the birds to separate them and secure
their feet. When the fishnet was untangled Lady Rose was
rushed to a corner of the bull pen for first aid.

We were next. It seemed as though Cush was betting
against the entire crowd. He took every bet offered. Hundreds of dollars were yelled back and forth. The man with
the little book furiously recorded the sums. When the betting slowed, the cocks were brought into the ring.

Cush turned to me. "This is what it's all about," he said
excitedly. "The moment of truth has arrived." Then he
waved to Otis.

The cocks were teased back and forth until the referee
and the shouting crowd thought they were sufficiently
heated up. Otis unleashed the leather strap and lofted Cash
forward. He went feet and spurs first into the feet and spurs
of the oncoming cock. It was a frenzied moment as men
hollered, Cush cheered, and the cocks went wild kicking
and slashing each other. Suddenly a thick spurt of brown-
ish blood squirted out of Cash's left eye.

"Time out," Otis shouted as he jumped into the circle and threw a net over the birds. Other men jumped in behind him.

"What happened?" I asked.

"I don't know," Cush shot back. "But it can't be good." He stood and waded down the bleachers as the crowd jeered him. Otis spoke softly to Cush. Cush was shaking his head, No, no, no. It seemed that Otis wanted to throw in the towel, but Cush wanted to continue.

Otis instructed his assistant to hold the cock. Then he stuck the entire bloody head between his lips. He sucked a mouthful of fluid from the eye and spit it to one side, then did it a second time.

"What's he doing?" I asked the man next to me.

"He's got too much blood in his head from the cut. It makes them dizzy. You got to suck it out so they can see properly," he replied. "It's a nasty business. But you either suck it out and let the cock fight on, or call it off."

Cush squeezed into the front row and rooted loudly when Otis lobbed Cash back toward the other cock. But he was done in. He flapped his wings a few times, tried to get his balance and flash his spurs, but then he just flopped over onto the dirt. The other cock strutted up to him and gave him a swift series of kicks. Otis threw the net over them. The crowd roared with approval and rose up to surround Cush.

"Okay, okay," he shouted. "Everyone form a single line and I'll pay out one at a time."

I thought of getting in the line along with everyone else, but I knew Cush wouldn't pay me. I had taken the risk along with him. Now I was a loser, like him.

Instead, I followed Otis back to where the trainers had set up the first-aid station. Cush's Cash was tossed onto a rough table. Blood drained out of his pierced eye.

"These belong to Cush," Otis said as he used a pair of pliers to twist the spurs off of Cash's legs. He tied a spur to each end of the thin leather strap and handed it to me.

"Thanks," I said. "What happens to the bird?"

"They're too tough to eat," he said brusquely, and in one motion he picked it up and chucked it over the stone wall.

I turned and walked across the bull pen. I passed through the little door in the gate and went around to the back side of the wall where Cash had been thrown. When I turned the corner I thought I was going to throw up. There was a pile of rotting and freshly discarded birds being clawed at by cats and mongoose. Feathers, bones, feet, and skulls were scattered across the spreading field.

That's what my big pile of money bought, I said to myself. A big pile of dead birds. I felt ashamed. I stooped down and picked up a few rocks. I threw them at the scavengers. They ducked and dodged, but they didn't run from me. I walked around the edge of the pile until I spotted Cash. A mongoose had already begun to tear away at his belly. Flies were settled on him like black sequins. It's a good thing you lost, I said to myself. If you had won, you'd be on the other side of the wall stuffing your pockets full of money and you'd never know that some other cock was back here with its guts ripped out. I reached over and pulled off a tail feather. I thought it would make a good bookmark in my diary.

I was sitting in the car when Cush stepped out the

wooden gate. His face was as red as the fighting cock's head. He was missing his hat, shoes, belt, and jacket. He pulled up his pants and stuck out his belly to keep them from sliding down as he walked forward.

"Hell of a day," he said, dropping onto the seat. "How are you holding up?"

"Drive as fast as you can," I replied. "I have a crazy feeling inside and I want to get rid of it."

"I got it too," he said and started the engine.

We drove up and down mountains, floored it on the straightaways, dodged goats, trees, cars, people, walls, and gullies. I suppose we could have been killed a dozen times and we still wouldn't equal the life of one fighting cock. Cocks were killed because of me and Cush and everyone else who was trying to make a fast buck. Betsy was right. I simply wanted the money and I didn't care how I got it. If I could have gotten the money without ever seeing the dead cocks, I could have lived with myself. I would have walked away, counting those tens and twenties. But I did see that pile of dead birds. And it was blood money.

When we pulled onto our street, he cut the engine and we coasted until Cush braked in front of the house before ours.

"You aren't angry with me?" he asked.

"I'm angry with myself," I replied. "And you stink."

Cush laughed. It didn't even bother him that I thought he was a jerk. "Ahh, don't take it so hard," he advised. "Easy come, easy go. That's how it is in a man's world."

I got out of the car, then leaned through the window on the passenger side. "I forgot to give you something," I said and reached into my pocket for the spurs.

He smiled. "I knew you wanted to get back in the saddle," he said happily and stretched out his hand.

Suddenly I changed my mind. "Forget it," I replied.

Keep the spurs, I thought. I paid for them. And if I kept them I'd know that some other cock wasn't getting diced up with something I bought. Then I walked away.

movie called "The day the Earth Caught Fire". It was about how the earth drifted too close to the sun. But the fires here were set by people with brains that have been fried under the sun.

Now the air smells like smoke. Our clot[hes] smell. And people only talk about It's as if we have a new kind of [weather]. Fire weather. Before it used to be a f[ire]

MASTERS
ARMY & NAVY
AVERAGE CONTENTS 49
SAFETY
MATCHES

MASTERS
ARMY & NAVY
SAFETY
MATCHES
CENTRAL MANUFACTURING WORKS LTD
CHAGUANAS TRINIDAD WEST INDIES

Fire

The fires started on the dry cane plantations toward the northern tip of the island. They were driven south by the Atlantic winds. Pete and I rode our bikes to watch the fire crews try to stop them. The flames leapt fifty feet into the air and tacked back and forth across the fields like blazing yachts. No one seemed terribly worried that they would get worse, and since the fields were so far away from the towns, it felt to me like a disaster taking place in California while I was living in Florida. When I asked Dad if they'd spread he replied, "They'll just burn themselves out. It's nature at work. The burned stalks fertilize the ground."

But they continued to spread. On nights when the winds shifted, the burning ash drifted across the sky like red eyes winking down on us. In the morning the roof, steps, windowsills, grass, and cars were all covered with tiny curls of black ash, like eyelashes. When I tried to pick up a perfect piece, it collapsed into a powder so soft I couldn't feel it, even when I rubbed it between my fingers.

When the fires popped up in odd places, the police and the fire department announced an arson epidemic. Someone was pouring gasoline on telephone poles and setting them off. Part of the Flower Forest was burned down, along with the tourist information booth. Abandoned houses were torched. Everyone was nervous. The front page of the newspaper showed a map of the island with wavy red flames printed where every fire had broken out. There were so many flames the island looked like a bird covered with burning feathers.

After dinner we were sitting out on the front porch when a taxi pulled up. The driver opened the back door and BoBo II hopped out and ran up the driveway. Mrs. Wiggins, who lived two blocks away, knew BoBo was our dog. When she caught him in her yard she sent him home in a taxi. Dad had paid the first three times, but not now.

"You can just return the dog where you got him," he said to the driver and pointed toward BoBo II.

The driver argued. Dad folded his arms and walked away. The taxi backed out of the drive and sped off.

"She's a drunk," Dad complained as he climbed the stairs. "She's three sheets to the wind by noon and can't tell the difference between a dog and a person."

"Let's go to the drive-in," Mom suggested and looked up at the dusky sky. The wind had shifted and the gray smoke and ash had blown out to sea like a cloud of gnats. "It will help take our minds off of things."

Dad took out his money clip and flipped through it. "Yeah, I could use a distraction," he agreed.

I ran to get the movie section out of his office before they changed their minds.

"We just missed the Jerry Lewis film festival," I announced when I returned to the porch.

"That's too bad," Mom said with a sigh. "I always get a kick out of him."

"He's an idiot," Betsy pronounced. "It lowers your IQ just to watch those films."

I gave her a look that was supposed to translate into: We're trying to be in an *upbeat* mood here.

She just smirked back at me.

I kept reading. "Seven-thirty, *Cool Hand Luke*. Nine-thirty, *The Comedians*. Eleven-thirty, *Don't Stop the Carnival*. One-thirty, *Island in the Sun*. Three-thirty, *The Wild Bunch*."

I looked up at Mom for a reaction.

"I've always liked Paul Newman," she said. "Let's catch the seven-thirty."

The Rudolph Drive-In was over by the airport. We got in the Opel station wagon, stopped by the Cheffette fast-food restaurant, picked up a bucket of chicken snacks, and arrived in time to get a good spot in the middle of the field and far enough away to easily view the entire screen from the backseat.

When the movie started, Paul Newman was already drunk and happy. He stood in a parking lot cutting the parking meters off their poles with a plumber's pipe cutter. I watched his face. He was *so* carefree and giddy. He was boozed up and couldn't feel a thing. He didn't care a wit for what trouble he was stepping into. It might matter later, but for now he was loaded and nothing could bother him.

But he was in trouble. In the lower right-hand corner of

the big screen, a flame popped up, having curled around the edge from where it started on the back side. Someone must have set it and run.

The flames confused me at first. They climbed up the edge of the screen so quickly and were so bright I thought I was suddenly watching a movie in 3-D. But it was real. Someone hit a car horn, then all the cars hit their horns and turned on their headlights, as though the extra light might douse the flames, the way turning on a light spoils a movie. But nothing stopped the screen from burning. The flames spread in ragged sheets up the front as the white paint bubbled and browned like grilled cheese. The movie kept running, and Paul Newman's drunken, carefree face was projected on the flames, so that his smile danced and shimmied as he laughed and dropped to his knees and giggled at something secret and uproariously funny, like a little devil with fiendish plans.

Around us, engines started and cars began to pull out like stampeding cattle. Dad stayed put. "We'll wait a few minutes," he said with his arms crossed. "Let them slug it out. We're far enough away from the screen."

Both the entrance and the exit were jammed up with cars in a panic to escape.

Dad shook his head as he watched the commotion. "Idiots" is all he said.

The screen was soon fully engulfed in flames. They leapt up the top edge like wild red hair. Newman's boozy eyes showed through. Whatever he felt, it looked good. He swooned and the screen swooned with him as it buckled, then split into pieces like a flaming jigsaw puzzle, collapsing on the ground beneath the twisted metal frame.

"Let's go," Mom urged. "It's too depressing just sitting here."

Dad started the car and we got in line. Slowly we worked our way out the gate. I looked back. I could see little bits of Paul Newman projected on a tree and part of someone's roof.

"Where's Jerry Lewis when you need him?" Betsy groaned.

"I heard he was in France," Pete replied.

Betsy shook her head. "You drive me insane," she whispered in his ear. He smiled.

Mom started giggling, then covered her mouth with her hand. "I shouldn't be laughing," she said. "I really hope no one was hurt, but that was the strangest thing I have ever seen."

Dad had been unusually quiet. Still, he had to get in the last word. "Things are really falling apart around here," he growled. "The whole place seems to be going to hell in a hand basket."

I glanced at Pete. He was looking at me with his finger over his lips. I knew what he meant. One wrong word and Dad would go up in flames. He had been upset for weeks and we didn't know why.

We found out why when some of Mom's friends threw her a party at our house. Mom was weeping even before the guests arrived. She was polishing a spot on the silver punch ladle when she turned to me and asked, "Don't you think Marlene would like the lawn chairs?"

"Sure," I replied. "Are we getting new ones?" I was puzzled because the ones we had were pretty new. But I knew this was not the time to ask why. She had a tissue tucked under the cuff of her sleeve and every few minutes she brought her wrist up to dab at her nose. She thought she was being sneaky, but the harder she tried to hide her feelings, the deeper I felt them.

"We're not getting new ones," she said. "We can't even pay for the ones we have."

How could that be, I wondered. We had two new cars. A new truck, a full-time maid, a laundry woman, a babysitter, a man to cut the lawn, and a chauffeur when we needed one. Pete and Betsy and I went to private schools. Mom and Dad had all their clothes and our clothes handmade. They were always out on yachts or at parties or dances. Dad worked and Mom worked. So how could things be falling apart? I knew I was going to have to ask Betsy, but it would have to wait until later. Mom's Swedish friend, Gunnie, had arrived along with Heather and Jo. Gunnie pronounced her name so that it sounded like *Gooney*. I liked her a lot.

"Jack," Mom said and wiped her eyes, "stay in the kitchen and keep the cat off the hors d'oeuvres while I get the door."

"Okay." I went into the kitchen wondering what was going on. Pete was already there. He was stealing hors d'oeuvres, then rearranging the platters so it wouldn't look like one was missing.

"Caught you," I hollered.

He yelped. "Don't tell Mom."

"Give me half." He held out a little piece of toast with cream cheese and red caviar. I took a bite, then licked the little eggs off my upper lip.

Mom appeared and almost caught me. "Go ask the ladies if they want a cocktail," she said, suddenly in a festive mood. I liked playing the bartender because I was good at mixing fizzy drinks. She sent Pete to his room to put on a clean shirt.

Mom followed me into the living room with a tray of hors d'oeuvres while I said hello, answered a dozen polite questions about my health and happiness, and took orders. Vera, Eileen, and Marie had also arrived. Gunnie took the tray. Mom hugged her friends, then followed me into the kitchen.

The cat, Celeste, was standing on a platter of hors d'oeuvres and lapping up the caviar. Mom let out a hiss and in one motion scooped up Celeste and tossed her out the open window. Celeste howled as she twisted through the air. Then we heard a second howl. A human howl. I stepped out on the landing and saw Celeste leaping from a man's head into the bushes.

Mom peeked out the window. "Oh my God!" she cried out.

"Are you Betty Henry?" he yelled, while one hand gently probed his scratched head. When he winced, I saw his teeth were mossy-looking, like rocks along the shore.

"I am," she replied.

He waved a manila envelope at her. "I'm a representative of the Caribe Collection Agency," he snarled. "I've come for our money."

Gunnie entered the kitchen and stood next to Mom and placed her hand across her shoulder.

"I'm sorry about the cat," Mom said nicely. "It was an accident . . ." She bit down on her lip.

"The cat's not the problem," he snapped, and kicked at the gravel. "Just give me the money you owe."

Gunnie turned to Mom. "I'll handle this vulture," she insisted, and pushed a curl of hair off Mom's forehead. "You go back with the girls and smile."

"I want the money," the man hollered. He was sweating down his face. His shirt was wet in wide stripes, as though he had leaned against a freshly painted fence. He had rolled the manila envelope into a tube and was beating it against the palm of his hand. "The law is on my side," he said arrogantly.

"One minute," Gunnie requested. "I'll be right back . . . Don't go away."

Wow, I thought. She's just going to whip out her wallet and pay for whatever he was asking.

Instead, she opened the freezer and pulled out a large bag of ice. "I'm coming!" she sang.

She lifted the bag with both hands over her tall hairdo and ran at the window. She threw it with all her might. He saw it coming and ducked. It hit the back of his shoulder with a loud crunch. He dropped to one knee, then popped up in a fit.

"You tried to kill me," he screeched. He pointed at me. "You're a witness. I'll drag you to court."

"Oh, shut up, you ugly bucket of worthless human scum," Gunnie shouted back. "Now beat it before I come down there and kick you over the fence."

He stepped back and hunkered down. "Oh yeah? Oh yeah? Well, we'll see who gets kicked around. By the time I'm finished, I'll kick those debtors off this island."

Gunnie grabbed the first thing in sight. She flung the

glass measuring cup. It sailed over his head and into the bushes.

He jogged a few steps down the driveway before shouting, "I'll get your cars, your house, your business . . . You'll leave here like rats fleeing a sinking ship."

"Damn him," Gunnie muttered. She grabbed the spatula and pushed past me and down the steps. He took off for his car. She chased him. He got there first and slammed the door. She swatted the window.

"If I ever catch you, I'll flatten your face," she hollered, and continued to swat the car like it was a giant fly.

He rolled down the window just enough so he could push the manila envelope out. "Debtors!" he spat, then sped away.

I hopped down the steps to retrieve the ice. It was all crunchy and just right for mixing drinks. I balanced it on my shoulder and returned to the kitchen. Mom passed by and tried to catch my eye. I kept turning my head away. I set my jaw a bit crooked and made the drinks.

After I had served everyone and made certain Mom didn't need me, I grabbed Pete and knocked on Betsy's door. Something was definitely going on and we needed to know details. Betsy always had the answers.

"It's simple," she said. "They spend more than they make and then Dad has been taking loans from the bank while business is dropping. Now the banks want their money and he doesn't have it. That's why he declared bankruptcy."

"Bankruptcy," I repeated. I only knew the word from playing Monopoly. It usually meant the end of the game, like when you rolled the dice and landed on Boardwalk and there was a hotel and you couldn't scrape up the rent. You turned in your mortgaged property and worthless single and five-dollar bills and went to bed a total loser.

"Does this mean we have to go back to Florida?"

"*You* will be going. I'm staying," she said firmly. "I'm tired of bouncing around. I feel badly for you boys, but if I don't get settled down now, I'll never get ready for college. And since I want to study in England the system here will help me. I'll miss you," she said, "but I have a scholarship to board and study at the school and I'm going to take it."

"You can't just leave," I said.

"Just watch me," she replied.

"But we depend on you."

"For what?" she asked sarcastically.

"To kick our butts day in and day out," I replied.

Before she could take that the wrong way, Pete began to giggle. She gave him her scorched-earth scowl. He took a step back and covered his face. "Watch out," he hollered. "She's a killer."

She jumped on him and wrestled him to the floor. Then she tickled him, kissed him, and tousled his hair. He made a sick face, but he loved it. One thing about Betsy, if she said she would take care of you, she would. She was like a pit bull. You might not want to hug her but you would want her around and you'd miss her if she left. She'd fight anyone and do anything to get things her way. Now she wouldn't have to fight us or Mom and Dad. She could just set her sights on what she wanted, then go get it. She was going to be living the life I wanted. And I was going to be living the life she was rejecting. I was so envious I had to walk away before I started to cry.

I returned to my room and took out my diary. Okay, I thought, you better start loading this up with Barbados stuff. It's now or never. It's over.

That night Mom and Dad argued. They were silent over dinner except to order us to our rooms once we had finished. As we walked off I steered Pete into my room.

"We'll ride it out in here," I whispered, even though the door was closed.

He nodded.

"It will be okay," I said.

The first words out of Mom's mouth were loud. "I was humiliated," she said bitterly. "You didn't tell me we were in so much trouble."

"How was I to know they'd send out a bill collector?" he replied. "I'll take care of it."

"How?" she questioned him. "And with what?"

"Don't start on that," he said.

I turned to Pete. "Stay here," I said and patted the edge of the bed as I reached under the mattress for my diary. "I'm going out there. I did this once before and it worked."

I slipped out into the hall and tiptoed down to where it opened onto the dining room. I stayed in the shadow, just by the edge of the door, and peeked out at them.

"This isn't just about me," Dad said. "You helped run up the bills."

"Oh no," she shot back. "Don't try to blame this on me. You were the one who set the pace. Spend. Spend. Spend," she hammered. "And then you tried to make it all work out by doing business on a handshake with a bunch of drunks who didn't have a cent to begin with."

Maybe it wasn't such a good idea to step between them, I thought. They might both turn on me. I still had time to retreat to my room. They hadn't seen me.

Dad paced back and forth. Mom continued. "And now you're becoming a rummy like the rest of them!"

"Damnit!" he shouted. I peeked around the corner just as he turned and rammed his fist through the glass door. It exploded into a thousand pieces and scattered like a bucket of marbles thrown across the porch and down the stairs.

Mom stood frozen, with her hands pressed over her ears. Dad stepped through the empty frame of the door and stomped down the stairs, kicking shards of tinkling glass out of his way as he went.

After the last bit of glass settled, I heard Hal Hunt's voice carried on the wind. "Did you hear something break?"

I scurried back to my room. Pete was still sitting on the edge of the bed. He was more frightened than I had ever seen him. I was more frightened than he had ever seen me. "Come on," I said. I grabbed his arm and jerked him forward. I opened the French doors and we ran out across the grass, through the back yard, to the garage. "Hurry. Hurry. Hurry," I cried out. "Get in."

I opened the side door and pushed him forward into the dark. "Get down," I shouted. "Stay down." I closed the door and shoved the bolt into place. Then I dropped on my knees and crawled next to him. We were breathing as if we had just run a mile.

"What happened?" Pete asked between breaths.

"Dad went berserk," I replied. "He punched out the front door."

In a moment I sat up and searched around. The garage was filled with empty cardboard boxes. I had seen this in the past and knew what boxes meant. We were definitely moving. Our stay in paradise was over. This was a bad ending to one of Dad's stories. What's the lesson, I asked myself. I just wasn't sure. Was it because Dad was bad at business? Was he a rummy like the rest of the men Mom disliked? I didn't know, and I couldn't ask him. He might go berserk again. I lay back against some boxes and thought, I'll never know why he failed. When I failed at something, it was because I hadn't paid attention or didn't prepare hard enough. But adults were different. They had problems I couldn't figure out. And I guessed that by the time I could figure them out I, too, would be an adult with the same problems.

Pete put his head on my shoulder.

"We'll be okay," I said. "We'll stick together."

"You bet," he replied.

After an hour or so, he fell asleep. I picked him up and lugged him like a sack of potatoes back to the bedroom.

In the morning Pete and I woke up acting like members of a retreating army. I opened one of my hollowed-out diaries and removed two packages of firecrackers. For once I agreed with Mom's favorite line, *If you don't use it, throw it away*. Only I added a twist to her thinking, *If you don't use it, blow it up*.

"Gather the stuff you don't want anymore," I ordered. "We don't want to leave anything behind."

Pete went into his room and returned with his plastic sailboat with ripped sails. "Blow it up," he said. "I don't want it anymore."

We took it out to the back yard. I taped a firecracker to the mainmast. Pete lit it and we stepped away. *Boom!* The mast split in half.

"Excellent!" he cried gleefully.

We blew off the rest of the masts, then the rudder and keel. After that, we tossed it into the trash. No one would ever play with that again.

I brought out a lamp made of a carved coconut. A few minutes later it was destroyed. Pete brought his old shoes and we blew the soles off. I blew up a math book. Pete blew up a mobile of painted fish which had been made out of mango seeds. With each blast, we jumped up and down and cheered.

When we were down to our last six firecrackers I said, "I know what I want to blow up."

Dad had painted our name "Henry" on a wooden plaque and wired it onto the front gate. I wrapped the remaining firecrackers into one big bomb and taped it to the plaque.

"Fire in the hole!" I hollered and lit the fuses I had twisted together. It went off like a truck backfire and echoed between the houses. The plaque blew in half. One piece stayed on the gate, the other landed in the street.

Pete put two fingers in his mouth and let out a long

whistle. "That is so cool," he said. "I wish we had some dynamite."

Just then a black panel van pulled up. The driver leaned out the window. "You guys know where the Henrys live?"

"Right here," I replied. "Why? You here to move us out?"

"Just the animals," he said, looking at a clipboard. "I'm from the Humane Society. Your mother called and said to come get the dog and cat. We'll find them new homes."

The Henry family retreat was under way. The enemy advance scouts were already on our doorstep. I reconnoitered the driveway. BoBo II was asleep in front of the garage. Celeste was sitting on the kitchen stairs licking her paws. I raised my head and looked up into the smoky sky. Oh God, I thought, I don't want to see this. But here it was.

The driver had also seen BoBo II and Celeste. He quickly got a butterfly net and two wire cages out of the van.

"Call the dog over," he said as nicely as he could, and put on a pair of heavy leather gloves.

"Can't do it," I replied.

He turned toward Pete.

"Me either," Pete said. "Not even if you torture me."

The man shrugged, then walked up the driveway. He went directly to BoBo II, grabbed his collar, then trotted him back to the cage. BoBo II went right in, and after circling around a few times sat down and stared out at us. Tomorrow he'd be sleeping twenty-three hours a day at someone else's house and never know the difference. There is an advantage to having such a tiny brain, I thought. There is no room to remember your past.

He picked up the cage and slid it into the back of the van.

"So long, fella," I said.

Pete began to cry.

"Hey," I said. "Better him than you!"

He turned and punched me in the chest.

Before I could punch him back, Celeste let out a screech. The guy had her half into the butterfly net. He was reaching for her with his leather glove when she broke away. She hooked him good across the nose, then leapt into the driveway and across into the Granthams' bushes.

"Go! Go! Go!" I shouted, and waved my fist over my head. I could see her working through the thick leaves and stems and then she was gone. Celeste was smart. She knew not to hang around us. I hoped she would run up into the hills and eat mice and live free. I wanted to run away and live with her. But the island was too small. Someone would find me, and just like BoBo II, I'd be sent home in a cage to face the music.

"It would be better if I had caught her," the man said when he returned to the truck. "Between the wild dogs and mongoose, she'll be killed."

"She's tougher than that," I said defiantly.

"Well, tell your mother I tried," he said and wiped a spot of blood off his nose. He put away the empty cage, then climbed into the truck and drove off.

That afternoon Mom came home with a set of new suitcases.

"Pack your good clothes and play clothes," she said,

meaning business. "We're leaving today. Your father will ship the rest up to us."

"Where are we going?" I asked.

"Miami," she replied. "We're leaving in four hours, now get a move on."

We each took a suitcase and dragged it to our room. I slipped my story diaries into my backpack. I could carry them onto the plane with me. They were the most important thing I owned. Once we were in Miami I could open them and read about where I had been. Then I would get new diaries and write about where I was going.

I only packed the clothes I still liked. When I finished, I dragged the suitcase out to the front porch and went to find Pete. He was with Betsy. She was packed up for boarding school. The baby was asleep in his crib. I half expected him to be packing up his little outfits. Betsy gave Pete a hug, then me. "Write me long letters," she said. "I'll write back."

"What about Mom and Dad?" I asked.

"Dad's going to stay until he settles the bills. Then he'll join you in Miami. Mom just wants to get a head start and get you boys in a new school."

I couldn't even think of a new school. Just the thought of meeting new people wore me out. I drifted down to my bedroom to rest. For the next two hours I just sat on my bed thinking of things I should do. I should write Mr. Cucumber a thank-you note. He was tough, but smart and fair. I should go say so long to the Naimes and Shiva and the Hunts. But I didn't. I just felt empty. Used up. Every time I thought of saying goodbye, I expected they'd ask "Why?" And I'd just throw up my hands and shrug.

"Adults," I'd reply. "I just do as I'm told and hope for the best."

Dad arrived and loaded the station wagon. He and Mom didn't speak. They seemed to communicate in grunts. Marlene had swept up the glass, but their feelings for each other were still smashed up. But they'd make up soon. They always did.

Pete and I took our seats. I was numb, until I looked at Betsy. She was crying. I waved, then sucked in my gut and held my breath until we were out of the driveway and around the corner.

At the airport, Mom, Pete, and I stood on the terminal balcony and waited for the jet to land. We watched it circle overhead, then turn toward the runway. But it dropped down too fast and hit the runway with a thud. The tires blew and the jet screeched up the runway, leaving two long black trails of smoking rubber. The ground shook as the jet slowly shuddered to a stop. Suddenly the hot tires burst into flames. The fire crews hustled onto the tarmac. They sprayed a swoopy circle of white foam, like whipped cream, over the tires and put out the fire. It looked as though the jet had landed on top of a birthday cake.

Above the fire crew, the jet doors swung open and orange plastic slides unfolded like enormous waking caterpillars. One by one the passengers slid to safety and ran through the foam toward the terminal.

"This is an omen," Mom murmured, shaking her head from side to side.

"What does it mean?" I asked.

"We shouldn't leave," she replied.

Just then, Gunnie rushed up to her. "We're throwing a

Betty can't leave party at our house," she gushed. "Come on."

Mom looked hesitant.

"It'll be fun," Gunnie said and reached for Mom's straw carry bag. "You could use a lift."

"Okay," Mom replied. "It doesn't look as if we're leaving."

Yes! We're staying. Mom and Dad will make up, and Dad's business will improve, and Betsy will stay with us, and if we hurry we can get BoBo II back, and I can get the Henry plaque back on the gate.

We rushed across the terminal and back to the parking lot. We hopped into the station wagon and suddenly everything was different. Dad wasn't scaring us. Everyone was happy at the same time. This is what's important, I thought to myself. Not *where* we live, but *how* we live. If we stuck together, I wouldn't care if we lived in a shack, wore rags, and ate lima beans out of a can.

Gunnie and her husband, Tim, grilled hot dogs and fish. They had a case of Lemon Squash and I ate and drank until I couldn't stay awake. I looked around the room. Mom and Dad were sitting together and laughing. Everyone was having fun. Things were returning to normal.

I slipped into the spare bedroom. Pete was already asleep. I lay next to him and conked out.

In the middle of the night I was awakened. "Let's go," Mom whispered. "They're waiting for us at the airport."

I was confused. "Huh?" I said sleepily. "What?"

She lifted me up by my arms and swung my legs over the edge of the mattress. "I have to get the baby," she said. "You wake Pete and get him ready."

"What happened?" I asked.

"They brought in new tires from Puerto Rico and the plane is ready," she replied. "Now hurry."

"I thought we were staying," I asked.

"That was just party talk," she said. "Wishful thinking." I wished it were true. "Where's Dad?"

"Asleep," she said. "Tim's driving us."

"Why?" I asked. Dad always did all the Dad stuff.

"He needs his sleep," she said impatiently. "He'll join us later. Now get going."

I helped Pete stagger out to the car. In a few minutes we were at the airport. The airline crew was waiting for us. We climbed up the stairs and entered the jet. As soon as we took our seats they closed the door and we taxied down the runway, turned, and took off.

Once we were up in the air I looked out the window. The sugarcane fires were still glowing. As we traveled far- ther away I thought Barbados would look frightening, as if we had just escaped a burning ship. But I was wrong. The fires stretched from coast to coast like party lights strung across the deck of a beautiful luxury liner. It wasn't the island that was sinking. It was us. The plane banked to the west. I looked out the window. The island was gone.

THE JACK HENRY ADVENTURES

By Jack Gantos

Newbery Honor author of the Joey Pigza books

Jack Adrift: Fourth Grade without a Clue
Jack on the Tracks: Four Seasons of Fifth Grade
Heads or Tails: Stories from the Sixth Grade
Jack's New Power: Stories from a Caribbean Year
Jack's Black Book

The five books in the Jack Henry series are partly based on the diaries I (like Jack Henry) started keeping in elementary school. Some might think I have filled my alter ego's world with oddball characters and strange situations, but to me the stories are mostly about the everyday stuff that went on in my family and in whatever nutty neighborhood we happened to be living at the time (we moved around a lot). I never thought I was special, because most of the kids I knew thought the world looked as loony and off-kilter as it did to me. Now, when I talk to kids about my family stories and neighborhood characters they still give me that knowing look which says, "The world hasn't changed that much." Weird stuff still happens to kids, and around kids. Weird stuff is everywhere. An eleven-year-old reader summed it up. After reading one of the books in the series, she wrote to say she had recommended the book to her friends because "Your stories are filled with the unsaid things that go on inside kids' brains." Who could argue with that?

—J.G.